Better than the Book

A Charitable Endeavors Novel

M.E. CARTER
ANDREA JOHNSTON

Better Than the Book

Charitable Endeavors #4

By M.E. Carter and Andrea Johnston

Cover design and Formatting by Uplifting Author Services

Editing by Karen L. of The Proof Is in the Reading, LLC

Front cover photo by DepositPhoto

Without limiting the rights under copyright reserved above, no part of this publication may be reproduced, distributed, or transmitted in any form or by any means, including photocopying, recording, or other electronic or mechanical methods, without the prior written permission of the author, except in the case of brief quotations embodied in critical reviews and certain other noncommercial uses permitted by copyright law. No part of this publication may be stored or introduced into a retrieval system or transmitted, in any form, or by any means.

This book is a work of fiction. Names, characters, locations, and incidents are products of the author's imagination or are used fictitiously. Any resemblance to actual events, locations, people – living or dead – is entirely coincidental.

The author acknowledges the copyrighted or trademarked status and trademark owners of various products, characters, businesses, artists, and the like which have been used without permission. The publication/use of these trademarks is not authorized, associated with, or sponsored by the trademark owners.

This ebook is licensed for your personal enjoyment only. This ebook may not be resold or given away to other people. If you are reading this book and did not purchase it, or, it was not purchased for you then please return it and purchase your own copy. Thank you for supporting this author.

Dedicated to Ambien and the chaos it brings.
Thanks for the inspirational stories.

Better than the Book

Chapter 1

Celeste

I come to awareness, peeling my eyes open slowly. Glancing around the room, I notice the sun isn't even up yet. I'm not surprised. I've been so stinking excited for the Prince of Darkness convention; I haven't slept well in days. Too much excitement and too many nerves. Because today is the day I will meet Hunter Stone.

He is the most amazing actor, even if he is on a stupid vampire TV show. Not that I have anything against paranormal stories.

Scratch that—I have a lot against storylines involving super long canines and sucking the blood of innocent young virgins. And yes, I know they aren't all like that. My blogging bestie, Carrie, has made me try enough different versions I recognize why it's a popular genre. But for me, it's a no-go. I mean seriously, why would anyone fall in love with Dracula for fun? I don't care how much he sparkles or whatever, a wooden stake is going right through his heart if one of those creepy creatures gets near me. Any other reaction is just stupid.

Not stupid, however, is Hunter Stone. Last year, I saw him in a tiny two-man show called, "Get Up," and I fell in love. Not actual love. Just actor obsession-love. Not actual obsession—okay, maybe a little obsession. He was nothing short of amazing in his role and I knew then he was on the cusp of greatness. If only he would have stuck to theater, there is no doubt in my mind he would be the future of Broadway. In my dreams, I would be right there with him, working backstage to help support his performances and bring them to life.

Except, he joined the cast of Prince of Darkness, the popular vampire cop drama on television. Do I hold a grudge that he gave up all he holds dear in the theater to run around with fake teeth?

Only a little. But I also get it. Being a working actor isn't easy. You take jobs you may not necessarily enjoy so you can eat. And if the opportunity to play a bit part to supplement your income comes along, you do it.

It's not Hunter's fault he's so damn good they made him a regular. Natural talent like his just can't be contained. In fact, they should be thanking him. He's the only reason I watch that dumb show anyway. Every week. Twice. I didn't even have a television until he joined the cast anyway. They owe him for my loyalty.

Fortunately, his role is still small enough that the add-on tickets I purchased to get his signature and a photo with him weren't too terribly expensive. I can't wait to show him the "Get Up" playbill I still have. While I don't keep a memento from every show I attend, it was truly a remarkable performance. In my wildest fantasies we'll bond over our mutual love of the theater and we'll start a beautiful friendship that turns into future collaborations. I've dreamt of it many times.

My dreams are over for the night now. There's no use in trying to get any more sleep, I might as well start getting ready for an epic day. I'd much rather be early than late and besides, I'm sure there are already people milling about the hotel before the convention starts. I don't mind doing a bit of people watching.

Rolling over, I place my feet on the small rug next to my bed and try to get my equilibrium to settle. I hate not getting enough sleep. It always makes me feel nauseous until I get moving. A solid eight hours of uninterrupted slumber is needed for me to function properly.

I take a deep breath and blow it out before making my way to the tiny kitchen Anna and I share. New York living is expensive, especially when you're just starting out. Stage Managing for small theatre companies doesn't pay much and while the blog I run with Carrie helps supplement my income, life in New York City is expensive. We all dream of a fancy apartment near Central Park, but my reality is, I share a matchbook size one-bedroom apartment in Brooklyn with my roommate, Anna Logan, known on the stage as Anna Kay. An aspiring musician, she's a great roommate and not just because she's super organized and clean but also very chill when she's home. She also travels frequently for gigs so we're not falling all over each other every day. Since our place is less than spacious, it's a win-win. Plus, she's always prompt with the rent. Really, I couldn't ask for more.

Except maybe for the stab of pain that hits my brain every time I take a step to stop. Oye. Lack of sleep is a killer today.

I get the old school coffee maker going and take a deep breath, willing my stomach to settle. Maybe a little pickle juice will help.

Sounds gross, I know, but my grandmother's favorite remedy always seems to work. Something about the vinegar balancing out an overabundance of stomach acid. I'm not a scientist so I don't know if there is actual proof this works on a scientific basis or if she was making up theories. What I do know is a jar of pickles is cheaper than a bottle of Pepto Bismol and bonus—it doubles as a snack.

Grabbing one of the four teaspoons we own from the drawer, I swallow the cheapy medicine and wait for my stomach to stop churning.

And wait.

And wait.

And suddenly…

"Oh shit." A dive for the sink and throw up everything in my stomach, which isn't much. The only thing I had last night was a peanut butter sandwich. It was much better going down.

This is bad. This is very bad. Pickle juice always works to stop mild nausea. What it doesn't stop, however, is full blown illness.

"I can't be sick. I can't be sick." I'm chanting as if I say it enough times, it won't be true, but suddenly my headache makes more sense. So do the shakes I'm feeling and the overall heaviness of my body.

As soon as the gag reflex calms down I rifle around the junk drawer looking for our thermometer. Since Anna and I share it, it only goes under our arm. Maybe not as accurate, but again… we're starving artists. We make do with what we've got.

"Deep breaths, Celeste." I follow my own instructions and breathe deeply. Maybe I can will myself into just being a little sick. Maybe I'm just pregnant.

That's it! I'm pregnant! It's been well over six months since I've been laid, and I can't exactly afford a baby on my tiny budget but, hey, there are sacrifices I'm willing to make so I don't miss this con. I have waited for too long to meet Hunter Stone. I will not miss out.

The thermometer beeps and I remind myself to add a degree. Wouldn't want the baby doctor thinking I'm too cold. That makes it…

"One hundred two point six!" I groan at my bad

luck before turning to upchuck in the sink again.

Looks like the only hunter I'll be coming into contact with today is me, as I hunt for some meds to kill this headache.

I'm bored. And lonely. And sad.

Once I finally finished throwing up and managed to get some medicine in me and keep it down, I accepted the truth—there will be no convention for me this year. What I could have pretended was food poisoning has morphed into the full-blown flu. Stomach and otherwise.

Part of me still feels like jumping out of this bed and going anyway. The other part of me knows I'll never make it without passing out in the cab. Plus, I don't really want to be known as the girl who gives Hunter Stone the flu. Yes, I'd like to make an impression and throwing up on his shoe would be memorable, but I'll pass this time. Me and my playbill will have to wait until next year.

I sigh deeply, disappointment running through me. There's only one person who will understand how I'm feeling right now and why. So I pick up the phone and call.

"Aren't you supposed to be on the road already?"

Carrie Myers knows me so well, as she should. We've been blogging together for years. It started as a hobby and turned into a way to make some extra income, thank goodness. Last month it paid my light bill. So we've been talking for at least an hour a week for years. She's like a sister to me. A sister who just reminded me why my heart is in tiny pieces all over my bedspread.

I open my mouth to respond but I appear to be getting worse so instead I cough, sniffle, and wheeze before finally sharing my heartache. "Should be. But I have stupid luck and woke up this morning with a one hundred two fever and a body that won't stop shivering."

"Oh no!" she exclaims. *Why does she sound winded?* "So you can't go?"

"And infect my celebrity crush?"

Another coughing fit takes over and I try to hack up a lung before continuing our conversation. Here I thought I felt bad this morning. Turns out it was adrenaline and excitement keeping me from hitting rock bottom. Once my dreams shattered, my body apparently when right down the tubes with it.

"I'm so sorry, honey. I know how much you were looking forward to this." I knew she'd understand. What I don't understand is why she sounds winded. I bet it has something to do with that weird squirrel of hers. Yes, I said squirrel. I don't get it. Squirrels are up there with vampires in my book. Both of which she loves.

"I know you're trying to make me feel better about the fact that I'm dying without ever meeting the man I've been crushing on for so long, but I don't think you do know how I feel. Have you ever had your dreams shattered and stomped on while you lie in bed and cough up a lung?"

"Where the hell is he?"

"Where is who?" My poor voice sounds all raspy and phlegmy. This just keeps getting worse.

"Did I say that out loud?"

"Yes, you did. And the fact that you didn't realize it means you're feeling frazzled. Tell me what's going on. Take my mind off the worst day of my life."

I suppose if missing a con is this life shattering, I'm doing pretty good. Tomorrow I will concentrate on that part. Today is my day to wallow.

"I can't find Luke."

As suspected, it's about the weird squirrel.

Another cough from me. Another sniffle. And finally the question I'm dying to understand. "How did you lose him? He's got the longest, bushiest tail ever. It's probably sticking out from under the couch now."

"I already looked there," she says, and I finally understand why she sounds winded. She's probably running from room to room playing hide-and-seek with a rodent. "At first I thought he was hiding, but now I bet he's sleeping somewhere."

I shake my head at the ridiculousness and immediately throw my hand up to my head. Bad idea. The extra movement makes my brain feel sloshy. Not a good feeling.

"You're the only person I know who would get

stuck housing a squirrel who has narcolepsy."

She giggles because she knows I'm right. "At least he's healthy. Doc saw him yesterday and gave him a clean bill of health."

I snort laugh, which is not a good idea in my condition. The pressure felt like I was trying to blow up my own brain.

"You just better hope that thing doesn't turn on you when he realizes he's an adult male squirrel and should be outside with the other rodents."

I can practically hear the eye roll from here. Carrie and I agree on most things. Rodents and vampires, not so much.

"If he was going to turn feral, he would have done it by now. Animals are smart. Some of them just know they'd never survive in the wild, so they adapt to living with humans. Oh here he is!"

"Where was he?" I ask, more out of curiosity than concern.

"From the awkward position he's lying in, looks like he fell asleep trying to build a nest under my pillow."

Ohmigod I want to throw up again. And because of the flu. "Eww. Yuck. He's on your pillow?"

"He was not on my pillow. He was under it."

"Suuuure. It took you three hours to find him. I'm sure he was on top of it, rubbing his little squirrel butt all over it before you found him."

"Yes," she deadpans, "because that's what they do. Rub their butts on things for fun. You're ridiculous, you know that?"

"Says the woman who lives with a rodent with a medical disability."

"Are you sure you can't go to that con? You're sounding awfully sarcastic for someone who claims to be sick."

"My pending death is making me pissy! Leave me alone!" I yell, which is a bad, bad idea. It immediately throws me into another coughing fit and now I have to pee too. This one takes way longer, and I'm surprised Carrie doesn't hang up on me. She's a good friend, like that. "I think I need to go lie down. Sitting doesn't agree with me," I croak and slowly push to the standing position.

"I think that is a very smart idea. Take a nap, and text me when you get up. I wanna make sure you're not dead."

"If you don't hear from me, tell my sister she owes my funeral a hundred bucks since she never paid me back for that pogo stick she bought."

She really does. It was during her alternative exercise phase and she was convinced jumping up and down on a stick had some sort of muscle building properties. That died a quick death when she ate it on the pavement her first time. Now she claims amnesia for her IOU.

"Will do. Love ya, friend."

"Back atcha."

I shuffle the twenty feet from the couch to my bed and climb in, tossing my phone on the small dresser beside me.

For just a minute I entertain the idea of trying to write the screenplay I've been working on. But I can't muster enough energy to grab it off my small nightstand before I'm asleep, dreaming of Hunter Stone's beautiful face and throwing up all over his shoe.

Chapter 2

Celeste

One Year Later

"I am so excited!" I singsong to myself as I do some last minute touches on my hair and make-up.

Today is the day I've been waiting for since my unfortunate flu last year. It is the day that I will finally meet Hunter Stone. I have tickets in my purse to prove it and have checked my temperature twice this morning to ensure I won't have a repeat of last year's fiasco.

Yesterday was actually the first day of the convention and while it was beyond amazing, it was a little, well, paranormal. It was a small price to pay to see so many of Hunter's new fans. His popularity has increased tremendously since his character is doing more on screen than nodding and showing his fangs. The world is seeing what I've always known—Hunter's talent is hard to ignore.

The only downside to this year's event is the steep price of the tickets I bought for a photo opportunity and autograph session. Those were more expensive than last year, but I have no doubt they'll be totally worth it.

Admittedly, so far, the entire event has been worth it. Even for a non-paranormal fan like me. There are all kinds of vendors in the lobby of the hotel selling swag and paraphernalia. And I had to have the super cute T-shirt I found with Hunter's face on it. Unfortunately, they didn't have a size that will fit my Double-D's, but my hunt is not over. I've got two more days to search the piles.

Once they opened the doors to the giant ballroom yesterday and welcomed us in, we watched some of the stars strut on stage and then listened to them talk about pranks on the set and the non-glamourous side of creating a TV show. The stage manager in me enjoys hearing what goes on behind the scenes of any production so I found it very interesting.

Not as interesting was the super fangirl who asked the first Q&A question, and promptly brought up the naked photo of the leading man that was leaked a couple years ago. It was obvious he was less than happy to be reminded of the encounter, probably because it was his ex-wife who was responsible for the incident during their dramatic and very public divorce. *Awkward.*

I have to hand it to him, though. He put on that actor mask pretty damn quick and told her off without actually telling her off. It was impressive. Maybe Hunter isn't the only phenomenal actor on this show.

Glancing at the clock on my wall, I realize I need to hurry. It's a five block walk to the subway and I can't chance being late. Photo ops start before the rest of the convention and I don't want to be rushed through my time.

Moving my partially written screenplay over, I grab my stuff, double checking to make sure not only are the tickets are tucked safely in my crossbody purse but also the "Get Up" playbill. I can't forget that. It's the whole reason I'm going. To get it signed and tell Hunter how moved I was during the entire show.

Content that I have everything I need, I head out of the loft and down the street.

It's a beautiful fall morning and I'm reminded once again that I'm blessed to be living in the city I love working in an industry I love. I may not be rolling in the dough and my diet may consist mostly of Ramen, but I never take any of it for granted. Living here, working in theater, my soul comes alive. To me, that's worth more than an apartment across the street from Central Park.

Adrenaline is pumping through my veins and my stride is less a stroll and closer to a power walk as I make it to the subway in less than five minutes, which gives me a solid ten minute wait for the train I need. I don't mind, though. This is one of the less stinky subway stops and we have a great sax player who busks everyday so there's entertainment while I wait. Someday I'll work on a show that needs his skills and you better believe I'll come back and encourage him to audition. The emotion that comes through his instrument, the way his whole body just syncs into the music—it's all just mesmerizing.

Sinking onto the bench, I flip open my notebook and double check my calendar for the day.

- 8:15 – Arrive at con. Browse vendor tables.
- 9:00 – Get in line for photo op in Conference Room 1. Try to be first.
- 9:30 – Photo op begins. Try not to sniff Hunter Stone.
- 10:30 – Q&A with cast members in main ballroom
- 12:00 – Break for lunch

I have a plan to maximize my enjoyment for today and it's all outlined right here in front of me. No deviations. I am going to have a great time today. I just know it.

Or maybe not.

I look at my watch and realize the train is already a few minutes late. That's weird.

Leaving my perch, I get closer to the flashing sign that suddenly shows…

"It's delayed?!"

You've got to be fucking kidding me.

It's okay Celeste. Deep breaths. It's just a one-minute delay at this point. I wait.

And wait.

And wait.

And then it happens. The sign changes again to just "delayed." This isn't good. Not at all.

Quickly, I grab my phone and pull open the app to see if I can get any more information. But of course all it says is "delayed indefinitely."

I clench my fists and my jaw in frustration. This is not what I need this morning. The longer I stand here waiting, the more I'm eating up the time I should be spending in line for my picture.

"Think, Celeste," I say out loud to myself. "Deep breaths and think."

The ferry! I can take the ferry across the river and grab the subway from there. Maybe I'll get lucky and the delays are specific to Brooklyn. It's worth a shot.

"Excuse me! Excuse me!" I shout as I try to race past all the other patrons who are probably heading for the river as well. It's not as slow going as it would be during rush hour, thank God for small miracles. But it's painful for my boobs. I went for a less supportive bra today because it looks so much better in pictures. In hindsight, I should have brought it with me and changed when I got there.

The race to the pier is about half a mile away. Even

at a quick pace it takes a while to get there. And of course as soon as I get there and find the right landing, it's pulling away.

"Dammit!!" It's an hour and a half wait for the next one. By the time I get to Midtown, the photo op will be in full swing. I could take the bus but with all the stops, that'll take as long as the ferry.

Wait. What if...

Maybe, just maybe if I use the car I keep solely to drive home once a year because insurance is cheaper than catching a flight, I can catch the tail end of the photo op and make the signing portion. It's worth a shot.

I race back out of the ferry station, pulling up the Uber app on my phone as I dodge the people mingling around like they don't have somewhere important to be. Seven minutes? How is that even possible? This is New York. I don't have a minute to spare waiting for an Uber, so I step up to the curb and hail a cab. The only car that pulls over is not as clean as I'd prefer but it's a sacrifice I have to make. Besides, it gives me a chance to check my subway app again which shows…

Delayed indefinitely.

Great. The subway is the fastest way to get around this city, so this sucks. At least it means I made the right decision grabbing a cab and not hoofing it back to the underground stairs.

Two miles and fifteen minutes later I hand my T-shirt money over to the driver and yell my thanks over my shoulder. Keys already in hand, I jog to my car. At least I'm moving it out of this parking space. It's been too long since I remembered to repark, and I can't afford a ticket for leaving it in the same spot on the street. I'll probably have to park six blocks away tonight, but it's the only way to keep a car in the city without paying a small mortgage for an underground garage space.

Climbing in, I toss my purse on the passenger seat, insert the key to turn the ignition and press the gas when…

Nothing. The car doesn't move. It tries, as indicated by the revving engine but it goes nowhere.

Throwing the door open, I lean out and sure enough, there's a boot on my back tire.

"NO, NO, NO!" I yell and bang my hand on the dashboard, as if I can beat the offending device off the wheel. I can't. Revving the engine again, I swear it moves even less than it did seconds before.

"Please Jesus, please let me get there. I promise Hunter isn't really an evil vampire sent straight from hell," I pray and take a few deep breaths in through my nose and out through my mouth. "I just want to tell him he's talented and good at his job. That's selfless and good, right? Please?"

I close my eyes tight and press the gas one more time.

Still nothing.

Dropping my head on the steering wheel, I take half a second to wallow in self-pity before running through my options. The subway is still closed so that's out. I can go back to the ferry but by the time I get there, I'll have to wait at least thirty minutes until the next one. And then when I get across the Hudson I still have to find a way to get to the convention hotel and if the subway is down over there too…

The realization hits me so hard it knocks the wind out of me.

I missed it. For the second year in a row all I have for my efforts are unused tickets, an old playbill, and shattered hopes and dreams.

Chapter 3

Celeste

One Year Later: Again

I look from the tickets posted on my corkboard down to my television.

The television I didn't even want until Hunter Stone joined Prince of Darkness.

The television I only use to watch Hunter Stone on Prince of Darkness.

The television that interrupted Prince of Darkness to warn us about an incoming hurricane. A hurricane that isn't scooting by us, dumping a bunch of rain. Nope. It appears this one is going to hit us head on. Now I know why its named Hurricane Chad—because this storm has douchebag written all over it.

I shake my head in disbelief. This can't be happening and yet I'm not surprised at all.

Sighing deeply, I pull up my email on my phone and tap, not wanting to know and yet probably needing to know.

And there it is. The email I was dreading.

Dear Prince of Darkness Participant,

We have been closely monitoring Hurricane Chad for the last several days and how it may affect the Prince of Darkness convention. Our number one concern has been and always will be the safety of our participants, staff, and stars.

After speaking with weather authorities in the area as well as city officials, we've made the difficult decision to postpone this year's convention.

At this time, please continue to hold on to your tickets as more information on refunds or transfers will become available…

I toss my phone aside, uninterested in anything else the email has to say.

I cannot believe I have missed my chance to meet Hunter Stone for the last three years in a row. Welp, that's it. It's over. As his popularity goes up, so does the cost of these tickets and I can't keep throwing cash at an event I won't ever get to go to.

It's official—I quit.

Chapter 4

Celeste

Januray in New York City is dreary at best. Not only is it typically the coldest month, you can bet any sucker it's going to rain or snow at least half the time and win. My umbrella and old rain boots become part of the entryway décor of our apartment. Not that we have an actual entryway. But you get my drift.

Needless to say, when Carrie invited me to her engagement party in Texas, I jumped at the chance to get out of the city and enjoy some warmer temperatures. When you're living through constant precipitation and gray clouds, mid-60s and sunny sounds wonderful. Oh, how I was mistaken. I was not anticipating the extreme heat and humidity.

Going from 29 degrees to a balmy 82 with 95 percent humidity is a huge shock to my system. When you have always been well-endowed plus, the boob sweat becomes real people. I had to put deodorant under the girls this morning to keep myself dry. It's not working. Thank goodness I brought more than two bras for a long weekend. This one is going to be a sweaty mess by the end of the night.

Carrie dances her way toward me, a huge smile on her face. Why wouldn't she be smiling? She is marrying one of the most eligible bachelors in the world of cover models.

Honestly, it still kind of blows my mind. I know I figured out she had a crush on him years ago, but it's still hard to reconcile that my friend, who has often shared very specific details of her latest book boyfriend, is marrying Matthew Roberts. The man who represents many of those same book boyfriends and is the leading man in many book nerds' fantasies. It's a little surreal. Most of all, it's amazing. Her fiancé is more than just abs on a cover. He's a great dad and loves my friend unconditionally. He has even accepted her affection for narcoleptic rodents.

Throwing her arms around me, Carrie pulls me into a giant sweaty hug. "I'm so glad you could make it. It's a long flight from New York City."

"Are you kidding? I wouldn't miss this shindig. I am, however, wondering how you live through summer around here. It's so hot."

Her eyes widen slightly like I've read her thoughts. "Isn't this weather weird? This is like the third time in history we've recorded temperatures this high in January. But at least it means we can enjoy the outdoors."

"You mean sweat my ass off?"

Carrie laughs, and I'm wondering if part of her delight is being drunk on love. "Just be glad you have curly hair. My hairdresser had to do all kinds of magic to make sure my hair doesn't frizz today. Matthew and I made sure to have contingency plans for rain and snow just in case, but it never crossed our minds to be prepared for a historical heat wave. So tell me—how is the screenplay coming?"

I should have known she'd bring that up. Ever since I excitedly told her I had a plot bunny in my brain and wanted to write it for film, she asks me about it regularly. Problem is, I've been working on it for over two years now and I can't seem to make it work.

It's not a hard plot line—an aspiring dancer trying to make it in the big city. Yes, it's reminiscent of all those 90s movies I loved growing up, but it's grittier. Harder. Truer to life as a starving artist who isn't a teenager living on a scholarship at a fancy school. In my brain it's fantastic. On paper—not so much.

I groan in response. "I never should have told you about that. If I ever attempt something like this again, I'll be sure to wait until it's at least close to being finished before telling anyone about it."

"I'm glad you told me, Celeste. It's your dream to get it written and produced."

"But today is about you, Carrie. You and your impending marriage to your dream man."

She glances around the outdoor space decorated with dim lights and flowers on every available surface. Sighing deeply as she no doubt takes a moment to absorb the romantic setting, she faces me with a dopey grin on her face. Yep. Drunk on love. This is the stuff romance books are made of, and it's her real life. For a book nerd, it doesn't get any better than this.

"It turned out really beautiful, didn't it? The party?" she asks, her expression turning wistful.

"It's absolute perfection. I've seen quite a few people talking about it on social media today. It's like the hottest event in the book world right now."

"You think?"

I look at her like she's lost her mind and point at the couple Matthew is talking to. "Your cover model boyfriend, sorry *fiancé*, is chatting up best-selling author Donna Moreno and NANA award winning narrator Hawk Weaver. Yeah. I'd say this engagement party is a big deal. By the way, why are the guys wearing those weird shirts?"

Both Hawk and Matthew have on black T-shirts that are covered in what looks like pictures of boutonnieres. The only difference is Matthew's says, "I am the groom" and Hawk's says, "I am not the groom."

"That's Hawk's thing." Carrie stares longingly at her fiancé. It's kind of nausea inducing, to be honest. If she really does eat him up like her face indicates she wants to, I'm outta here. "He buys these ugly shirts for charity or something, and since Matthew loves charity as much as the next guy, he always requests one whenever they see each other."

She giggles. Carrie actually fucking giggles. People in love are so weird.

Suddenly she gasps and grabs my arm. "Did you see what Matthew got me for our honeymoon? Tickets to Australia! Can you believe it?"

"I actually can. I'd have to put a stop to this relationship if he didn't realize it would be the perfect place to spend a couple weeks consummating your new marriage."

Carrie's face turns a bright pink and my eyes widen.

"Carrie Myers, you bad girl," I chide playfully. "You gave up the goods already."

She flips her dark hair over her shoulder and tries to play off her embarrassment. "We are engaged. It's almost like being married."

"Oh no, it is not," I say with a laugh. "But I'm not judging you. The whole point of your celibacy was to make sure the next man you were with was completely and utterly serious about you, no matter what. I think waiting for over a year to get in your pants and publicly humiliating himself to propose means Matthew's pretty solid."

I shudder when I think of the dance I watched him perform for his proposal. He may be a decent dancer in pants, but in heels? Not so much.

"Yeah. Oh hey," Carrie blurts out shifting gears, "did you get your tickets for the con sorted out?"

Taking a sip of my wine, I shake my head. "Nope. By the time I stopped getting glitches on their website so I could register for the events I wanted, they were at max capacity and gave me a refund instead."

Carrie gasps. "Oh no! Did you email them? Fight with them about it?"

I shake my head, mostly in frustration from even thinking about the shitshow this convention has become to my life. "I didn't even bother."

"Why?" she whines. "You've been trying to get there for three years. You deserve to go."

"Exactly. I've tried for three years and something always stops me at the last minute. Clearly the universe is trying to tell me something and I don't have it in me to be disappointed again."

"Disappointed about what?" a deep voice asks, interrupting our conversation. I guess I should give him grace. He is the groom-to-be.

Carrie wraps her arms around her man's waist and proceeds to answer for me. "She's been trying to go to the Prince of Darkness con for a few years and every time she buys tickets, she ends up having to cancel last minute."

"Because the universe doesn't want me to go," I insert, not that I'm bitter or anything. I'm more like trying to keep a silver lining or something.

"Or it could be coincidence," she argues back and turns to look up at Matthew. "She's been a huge fan of Hunter Stone since she saw him in some off-off-Broadway show."

"Hunter Stone?" Matthew sounds confused, but I'm not sure why. Hunter is practically a household name these days. "I just had that cover shoot with him a few weeks ago. We hit it off. I bet I can just ask him for some passes."

He looks down at his phone, completely oblivious to the fact that my jaw has just hit the floor. Matthew knows Hunter? My blog partner's fiancé is friends with my celebrity crush? How is this happening? More importantly, how did I not know this sooner?

"Oh, I forgot about that!" Carrie announces, and I throw my hands out.

"You forgot? How could you forget about something like that? That's like me forgetting that, that… that you have that weird squirrel or something."

"Luke is not weird," she shoots back. "Just disabled. And I didn't think about it because it was like a one-day job while we were in the middle of a busy season or something. Matthew didn't even leave town for the shoot."

I open my mouth to keep playing this tit-for-tat game with her, but Matthew speaks before I can argue.

"Done. You have tickets to… hang on…" He zooms in while I blink rapidly a few times, in serious disbelief that this is happening. "Looks like it's an all access pass to the event, all the pictures, autograph signings, and one round-table of your choice. Will that work?"

I'm not sure how it's possible, but my jaw drops even further. I turn quickly to Carrie and point at her. "If you don't marry this man, I will."

She looks up at Matthew and makes what can only be described as googly eyes at her fiancé. "Don't worry about that. I can't wait to be Mrs. Matthew Roberts."

He makes a sound that can only be described as a grunt, and then leans down to gently take her lips with his. And they kiss.

And kiss.

And kiss.

And as fun as it is to read about, standing two feet away from them while they make out is not the same.

"Okay, so I'm wildly uncomfortable now. I'm going to get another drink. You guys… just"—I wave a hand at them—"carry on or whatever."

They don't even notice when I walk away. Not that I expected them to. If he's finally getting all the sex, I applaud their ability not to disappear in the middle of this party.

Sidling up to the bar, I wave the bartender down.

"I'll take another pinot, please." He nods at my request and turns away to hopefully fill the glass to the top this time. While I wait, I open my email app and sure enough, Matthew has already forwarded me a message from someone at the con asking for verification of my information for the VIP tickets.

I can't believe I have scrimped and saved and spent three years trying to meet Hunter Stone. Yet Matthew sends one quick text and suddenly I've got the most expensive passes money can buy at my disposal.

Not that I'm banking on using them. The universe has a funny way of shutting me down at the last minute. So as excited as I should be, I'm not. I'll believe this miracle when I see it.

Chapter 5

Hunter

When did I get this old? Or rather, when did I start looking this old?

The fine lines around my eyes, the same ones my mom says are from smiling, are more obvious than a year ago. If I lift my brows, my forehead crinkles and, while a few years ago they went away quickly, now, they linger. Maybe it's exhaustion and not aging.

I'm exhausted. Beyond exhausted, actually.

For years, I studied and honed my craft. Learning from anyone who would teach me, asking questions, and taking any gig—paying or not—to put my efforts to work. Off-off-off Broadway, also known as dinner theatre in a former pizza place, may be where I started but it isn't where I sit.

Now, I'm one of the most sought after actors

around, thanks to my big break with Prince of Darkness. The announcement that our little television show was going to be turned into a feature film catapulted those of us who could still stop by the local market for a frozen pizza into pseudo stardom. That doesn't include the film I co-starred in last year that's scheduled to release for spring break. When I signed on, I had no idea our little action film we had so much fun filming would be touted as this year's "Blockbuster to Beat." The response has been overwhelming to say the least.

"Sir," the chipper voice calls out, pulling my attention from the mirror. I turn to face the kid who has been assigned as my handler for the day. Dressed in a pair of skinny jeans the color of an eggplant, he's sporting a pair of glasses that used to be popular in the eighties. Grinning from ear to ear, he's also bouncing on the balls of his feet. When I first introduced myself to him he went on and on about my co-star, Penelope Warner. I can't blame the kid, she's gorgeous. A bit of a hard-ass but beautiful, nonetheless.

"What's up?"

"I've been asked to tell you we're only five minutes from your announcement."

Nodding my head, I move toward the door to the small bathroom attached to the green room my co-stars and I are using as our "safe space" this weekend. My how times have changed. Three years ago at this convention I could have roamed the aisles like the attendees and used the public restroom like any average guy. Now, I'm hiding out in the green room until security is ready for us to move.

Taking the last few minutes of down time, I splash ice cold water on my face, hoping to reduce the puffiness under my eyes, and waking me up. It's go time and it isn't fair to the people who have spent their hard earned money to meet me if I'm not fully "on." I hate that term but that's what it is. I turn the actor persona on and off regularly.

With fans and the press, I'm expected to be all smiles and conversational. Charming and witty. Everything I'm not unless there's a script and director involved. Growing up in a large boisterous family I was never one to fight for attention. Desperately shy and introverted, I sat on the sidelines while my siblings and cousins bantered and roughhoused. Preferring to be an observer rather than a participant, nobody was more surprised than I was when I fell in love with theater.

Classmates swore drama was the road to an easy A in high school, so I marked it as my elective freshman year and, like they say, the rest is history. I was bitten by the acting bug after only a few weeks and, while I spent the first year as part of the ensemble, I was determined to learn and succeed.

Patting my face with a paper towel, I take a deep breath and slowly exhale. It's a few hours. I can do this. Turn on the charm, take some photos, and thank every person who waits in line for the thirty seconds the organizers allow them to speak to me. That's why I'm here. Why I do this. For them.

Once the last photo is snapped, I'll slip back to my

dressing room and recharge. Let my mind settle and get ready for the second half of the day. At least during that time, I'll be with my castmates and the attention will be on them too.

Exiting the bathroom, I stop in front of the kid who hasn't moved since I went into the bathroom.

"How do I look… what's your name?"

"Andy, sir."

"Not sir. Just Hunter. Do you think I'll get a bunch of shit for not dressing up?"

The kid looks me over. What is his name? I know he just told me and yet, my mind is blank. Ask me to repeat the monologue that got me accepted into my first acting class and I wouldn't hesitate. But, remember the guy who is keeping me on schedule for twelve hours today? Not a clue. Assessing my choice of attire for this occasion. I'm not only dressed down, but it's a look my character would wear so it seemed like a reasonable choice. Dark wash jeans and a black T-shirt with a pair of well-worn motorcycle boots to complete the look. Really, I didn't have the energy to think outside of a pair of jeans and a T-shirt.

"Nah. You've got that brooding vampire look going. Seems on brand."

On brand? Who is this guy?

"What do you know about brand…?"

Following him as we exit the room, I nod hello to other actors in the hallway as I fall in step and wait for him to tell me his name.

"It's Andy and I'm a business major with a minor in marketing," he replies casually, seemingly unaffected that I can't remember his name. It gives me a twinge of guilt that he's used to actors blowing him off so I make a mental note to try harder. Just for today.

"And you think my brand is brooding?"

Snorting a laugh, he shakes his head before saying, "I think that's what the public believes to be true. Whether it is or not isn't for me or anyone else to decide. It's the perception."

"Well, the perception is wrong. I'm not brooding. I'm fucking exhausted."

Pausing at the door to the small room I'll stand in for the next few hours, my handler turns to me. His expression is a little patronizing but also sympathetic. "If I've learned anything working at these events, there isn't much of a difference. There are a few waters in there on the table and I'll be in the room should you need anything. We'll hand you whatever needs to be signed and when you've got your John Hancock on it, we'll take it from you to keep moving things along. About halfway through, we'll take a short break so you can regroup and hit the bathroom. Cool?"

Speechless at how this kid, who can't be more than twenty-one years old, seems to have this business all figured out and can keep us on track for the purpose of this day, I simply nod.

"Show time."

Taking in a long breath, I exhale and turn "on" my work persona before entering the room.

I should have asked… damn, I really need some sleep. I still can't remember his name. "Handler" seems like a great alternative. I should have asked Handler to work in at least two breaks today. The fans have been great, making me laugh and even embarrassing me a little with their requests. I've signed everything from glossy photos to T-shirts and canvas bags. One woman, at least seventy years old, insisted I sign the back pocket of her jeans. When she shimmied her rear in my face as I tried to scribble my name, I was both entertained and mortified. She, was neither. Proud and flirtatious was more how she felt.

Glancing down at the first major gift I bought myself that proudly adorns my wrist every day, I note there are only about twenty minutes left in this session. I'll have a little time to relax and get my mind ready to finish out this day with a big smile on my face.

Uncapping my water, I lift the plastic bottle to my lips as the next person steps up. The first thing I notice is the pile of blonde curls and big brown eyes that are the size of half dollars as she approaches me. A dazzling grin is spread across her pretty face, one I return as I recap the bottle. Then she stops.

What is she doing?

Looking into the large bag crossed over her body, she's mumbling, and I think cussing herself out as she rummages through the satchel. Tilting my head, I watch her, fascinated as she appears to argue with herself. Just when I think she's about to give up on whatever it is she's searching for, she lets out a squeal and lifts her eyes to me.

"Hi."

That's why I get paid the big bucks. I'm full of all the great lines.

"Hi. Oh wow. This is happening. Holy shit. Oh! Sorry."

Chuckling at her word vomit, I lift a brow and immediately regret that as thoughts of my forehead creases comes to mind. "What's happening?"

Her cheeks pinken as she gets closer to where I'm standing. "This. You. Here. Ohmygosh. I'm sorry. I'm not normally this weird. Hi. I'm Celeste."

Extending my hand, I introduce myself. "Hunter Stone. Thanks for coming today. I hope you weren't waiting too long out there."

"Nope. I actually just got here. Thanks for the VIP pass, by the way."

VIP pass? Who did I give a VIP pass to?

It takes a few beats before her words make sense. My new buddy, Matthew, reached out to me a few weeks ago for a pass to this con and I'd completely forgotten about it.

"Oh, you're Matthew's friend. Nice to meet you."

"Celeste. I already said that. Shit. Sorry," she

rambles before finally catching herself and her word vomit. "I wouldn't say I'm Matthew's friend, but he is marrying my best friend, so I guess we're going to be friends by marriage."

Pointing at the plastic in her hand I inquire, "What do you have there?"

"Oh!" she shouts. The room we're in is small which makes the sound much more amplified than one would expect. "Sorry," she whispers.

I'm not. This woman is hilarious and a breath of fresh air. She seemed a little nervous when she walked up but no longer. I realize I've been smiling the entire time I've been talking to her. Not the actor smile but the real me smile. Natural and sincere.

The calm I feel around her overrides Handler's impatient toe tapping. I know it's his job to keep us on track. And I know this interaction is taking longer than he deems appropriate. I just don't care.

"It's a playbill. I've been following your career for years. I saw 'Get Up' three times in the six weeks it ran and knew one day you'd be here. Well, not here here. I mean, if you'd asked me then I never would have guessed you'd be playing a vampire on television. A duke or earl in a period piece? Absolutely. A vampire? Nope."

Blown away by her declaration, I open and close my mouth a few times before gathering my wits to ask, "You saw 'Get Up'?"

"Yep. I've been saving this playbill for years. Will

you sign it?"

Looking down at the table where she's placed the aforementioned yellow pamphlet, I note she never relinquished control of it to any of the volunteers *and* has it safely secured in a plastic sleeve. Wow. This woman is serious about her memorabilia. Cautiously, I slide the playbill from inside the plastic and quickly thumb through the pages. Nostalgia hits me. This little production was one of my first when I arrived in New York. I had less than no money, but I knew this was where I could learn the most. I shacked up with four other actors in an apartment no bigger than a postage stamp and paid the bills by bussing tables and walking dogs.

It was a struggle but still some of the most fulfilling years of my life. Scribbling my name across the front, I carefully return the item to the plastic sleeve as— Andy! Like in *Toy Story*. Thank goodness I'm not losing my mind completely. *Andy* clears his throat from behind me.

"Oh shit. I've been in here too long."

"It's okay," I reply with a wink. "You have the special VIP pass. Besides, I know a guy who will make sure you don't get in trouble."

Celeste's cheeks redden at my poor attempt to flirt. Not that I'm trying to flirt but sometimes I slip into character without even realizing it.

"I better scoot. Thanks for signing this."

I watch as she walks away and, for the first time all

day, I feel the exhaustion melt from my muscles. See-ing that playbill has reminded me of why I'm here and all I've accomplished.

Chapter 6

Celeste

I look down at my map of the hotel again and back up to the numbers on the wall. This hotel's layout is so confusing. I'd probably know my way around better if I'd stayed here but I used all my points to book the cheapy flight from La Guardia to Chicago specifically for this weekend and didn't have any left over to splurge on a swanky place like this. Besides, the Motel 6 by the airport is still bigger than my apartment, so it's fine for sleeping. And Chicago has a great bus line that is a little slow but is easy to use. It dropped me off just down the block this morning.

My confusion isn't helped by the fact that the next event on my agenda is the one I'm most nervous about—a private meet and greet with Hunter Stone and eight of his biggest fans. Or at least the fans that were willing to shell out a shitload of money to chat with him for forty-five minutes.

Usually there is a lottery or something to even have a chance to buy one of these tickets, so you can imagine my shock when I found out it was included in my pass. The lady at registration explained I didn't just have a VIP pass. I had an "Actor's Guest VIP." It gives me access to everything. Even backstage and the green room. No way I'm taking advantage of those perks. I had a hard enough time talking to Hunter Stone for thirty seconds after spending an hour working on breathing techniques. I'm staying out of any areas where he may pop up and conversation has to be ad libbed. I'll just gather my free T-shirt and call it a win.

Later, of course. I'm not missing the chance to chat with him during this meet and greet.

A convention volunteer—I only know that because she's wearing the white shirt and black slacks uniform they're all wearing—steps out of the room I'm walking past and we almost collide.

"Oh! I'm so sorry. I was looking down at my map," I apologize. "I can't seem to figure out where I'm supposed to be."

She smiles kindly, like me getting lost is the most normal thing in the world. "This hotel isn't set up well if you're trying to get multiple places back to back. Which room are you headed to?"

"Um…" I look back down at my itinerary to quintuple check I have the right room number. It does me no good if I tell her the wrong thing and end up on the other side of the property. "Four thirteen D."

"You're in luck." She points to the placard on the wall. "It's right here. The Hunter Stone meet and greet?"

"Oh good." I let out a breath of anxiety that had been blooming in my chest. "I was so worried I'd be late."

She grabs a clipboard off a small table next to the door and begins flipping through pages. "Nope. You're the first person here. I like it when people are punctual. Especially since I can already tell who is going to come racing in at the last minute." Finding the page she was looking for she adds, "Can I see your badge please?"

I hold out the badge given to me at registration with my name, picture, and level of ticket on it. The organizers went all out with the fancy tags and lanyards. This sucker is even laminated. Of course with how expensive it would have been to purchase if I didn't "know people," they better provide fancy little perks.

"Okay, Celeste. Thank you so much." The volunteer, whose name is Klarissa judging by her name tag, drops the clipboard and picks up a paper bag, shaking it. "When you go in the room, there is a round table with ten chairs. Each chair is numbered randomly. Whatever number you pull out of this bag, that's the chair you are to sit in. Make sense?"

I snicker. "That's to make sure there aren't any cat-fights over sitting next to the star, isn't it?"

"Smart and prompt. You may be my favorite fan

yet."

Klarissa holds out the bag and I dig in, not having any real preference on where I sit. If I'm across from Hunter Stone, I'll be able to make eye contact. If I sit next to him, I'll be able to smell him. Actually, that's probably a bad idea. Being in his presence already made me fumble my words. I don't need to fall out of the chair too.

I pull out the square paper and hand it to Klarissa. "Number nine! Head on in and make yourself comfortable at the number nine chair."

I do as instructed and enter the room, leaving her to deal with the other fans that have finally found the room. Locating my assigned seat, I settle in and wait, content to go over my schedule once more.

- ~~11:30 – Meet and Greet with Hunter Stone in room 413D. DO NOT BE LATE.~~
- 12:15 – Short lull to shop and grab lunch. Must get free t-shirt then.
- 1:00 – Meet in convention hall for panel discussion with writers and directors. Take notes.
- 2:00 – Photo op with Hunter Stone in room 123A. DO NOT BE LATE.
- 3:30 – Meet in convention hall for panel discussion with actors. Unknown if Hunter Stone will be there. Arrive early for a close seat.

Content that everything is in order, I flip the page of my notebook to one that is blank and ready for me to take notes. Sitting back in my chair, I cross my ankles and watch the others as they begin to file into the room. So far, eight of the ten chairs are filled. That means either Hunter Stone will be sitting right across from me, or…

Right next to me.

Deep breathes, Celeste. He's just a person. The most talented, super-hot person. But that's beside the point. Stay focused. Concentrate on the older woman on the other side of the table. Why is she wiggling her ass at us? Is that… yep. Someone signed her ass. Poor bastard.

Suddenly, another woman, because that seems to be the vast majority of the convention participants, comes racing through the door.

"I'm so sorry I'm late," she says through deep pants. "I got chatting with Michael Ornaste and, well, you all know how he is when he gets going."

The other women nod their heads. I, on the other hand, have never met the star of the show so I wouldn't know how long-winded he may be. But I am wondering how I ended up with the guest pass and she didn't if she knows him.

Glancing up, I catch Klarissa's eye and she gives me a look that screams, "I told you so."

I don't have time to respond though. A young guy with weird 80s glasses comes sauntering and behind him…

Holy shit, Hunter Stone is here.

And why do I keep referring to him by his full name?

That's weird. Stop it, Celeste.

I will my brain to quit calling him by his full name and my heart to stop beating erratically by continually reminding myself he's just a man. The man of all my theater-loving fantasies, but a man, nonetheless.

"Hunter!" the woman who arrived late says as she immediately wraps her arms around him, pulling her flush against her. Hunter Sto—*Hunter* doesn't resist which makes me wonder, yet again, how I'm the one with the guest pass.

"Martha," he greets kindly, his arms draped around her. I've never been jealous of another woman getting a hug, but I admit, the feeling is running through me right now. "How long has it been? A month since the last con?"

"You remember." Martha is clearly delighted. "St. Louis. And a couple months before that in New York. And don't forget San Antonio."

"I couldn't forget San Antonio if I tried. I think that's the first time you ever came to my meet and greet."

"And you haven't been able to get rid of me since."

They both laugh as Hunter Stone turns to the table, his arm still over Martha's shoulder. "I think Martha here holds the record for attending the most consecutive Prince of Darkness conventions in history. What, eight so far?"

She nods proudly. "Hoping to go for a solid twelve this year, so you'll be seeing me around for a while."

Hunter Stone smiles and takes a few seconds to look at every single person sitting at the table. He misses no one, making sure to catch each person's eye. It feels very personal. Intimate. I'm impressed by the effort it takes to give everyone that experience.

And then his eyes catch mine and they flicker in recognition. One eyebrow raises slightly as his lips slowly lift into a smirk. A flutter settles low in my belly at the idea that he's recognized me. Of all the hundreds of people he's met today, he remembers me.

Matthew. He knows Matthew. It is a mutual friend recognition not about me. *Of course*.

Clearing his throat, his eyes skirt the room. I note the moment he spots the empty chair next to mine. Releasing a reluctant Martha, he shifts out of her personal space and makes his way my direction. Or rather, the direction of the empty seat. Clapping his hands together his voice commands our attention "Alright ladies, my handler over there says we've got thirty-five minutes for chitchat so what should we talk about?"

Hunter Stone pulls the chair out and sits gracefully, but in a manly way. There is no lack of confidence in this guy. Why would there be? With dark, ink-black hair and stunning green eyes, he's absolutely irresistible. In the business-sense, of course.

What is not at all business related is whatever cologne he's wearing.

Dear Lord, do not let me pass out from how delicious he smells.

But of course before I can pull myself together, he turns and looks right at me. "Celeste, right?"

I know my eyes widen because he laughs at my reaction. Laughs! If I wasn't trying to make a good impression I might smack him, but I'm too flattered he remembers my name.

"Um, yes. I can't believe you remember."

"It's not everyday someone remembers my very first performance on a New York stage."

"That was your first role? That's... incredible. I knew you were talented but to come out of the gate with a performance like that. Well, it's no wonder Hollywood snatched you up."

For just the briefest of seconds, his expression darkens, like he's having memories he doesn't particularly care for. But it's gone just as quickly as it came, and he barely misses a beat in the conversation. "Do you live here in the city?"

I shake my head. "I used some miles to get here. I live in New York. Brooklyn, actually. Close enough to get to any theater in the city in a reasonable amount of time, but far enough from Manhattan I don't go homeless."

His head cocks to the side. I can almost see that he

has a million questions running through his mind. Or maybe I just have a million running through mine.

"So you really are a theater buff."

"Stage manager, actually. I haven't done Broadway yet, but I'm up for a second assistant stage manager in a huge production that starts this summer. I haven't heard back yet, but fingers crossed." Like an idiot, I cross my fingers. "And I run a blog with my best friend, Carrie. She has a pet squirrel which is a story for a different day, but yeah. I cover theater and movies on the blog. Lots of critiques. Of course I always recommend your stuff. It's always so good…"

My words taper off as I realize I'm not only babbling; I'm taking up time that needs to be spent with eight other people.

"So, um, yeah. That's it for me."

Hunter Stone nods. I really need to stop using his full name. I don't even know another Hunter. But, it just rolls off my tongue so easily. "Thank you for that, Celeste. I love meeting fellow theater nerds."

My breath hitches at the word love. Not because he loves me. Because that would be stupid. He doesn't love me. I mean, he probably does in that he's-a-human-I'm-a-human kind of way, but not love, love. Oh boy. I'm losing it.

For the next half hour, I sit quietly as Hunter Stone makes sure to speak with each participant one by one, asking where they're from and their favorite story lines. His ability to engage every single person in the room, handler included, is amazing. He makes everyone feel welcome, everyone feel important. He has more charisma in his little finger than I do in my whole body. Without a doubt, my professional crush on a colleague's talent is quickly turning into a full blown romantic crush on the actual man. I'd call myself out on it except there are worse people to be attracted to.

"Five minutes," the volunteer handler calls out and everyone shifts in their seats expectantly. Everyone except me. It appears I'm the only one who hasn't been in a meet and greet before and I have no idea what's happening.

Hunter Stone pushes his chair back and stands. "Anyone want to take a selfie before we go?"

Immediately everyone is out of their chair and standing in a short line, phones ready to hand to glasses man for optimum photography. There are conversations with Hunter Stone, pictures, and lots of hugs.

Unfortunately for my schedule, but maybe fortunately for me, I'm the last one in line.

"I'll take your phone," Glasses demands more than offers. By the way he keeps looking at his watch, their schedule is probably tighter than mine.

I hand it over and Hunter Stone puts his arm around me. Me. Celeste Pumperkin is wrapped up in Hunter Stone's arms and if I die right now, I will die happy.

With my face next to his shoulder, I'm close enough that I swear I hear him sniff my hair. I'm probably imagining things, but since I just did my own quick sniff of his neck, I'm not judging. No, I'm smiling as Glasses says, "One, two, three… and again one, two, three. Here ya go."

He practically throws my phone at me and I know it's time to go.

"Thank you, Hunter Stone."

A deep, masculine chuckle rumbles through him. "It's just Hunter."

Embarrassed, I tuck a stray hair behind my ear. "Sorry. I call you that in my head and it's hard to change when I say it out loud. Thank you… Hunter."

"I don't mean to interrupt"—although the look on Glasses's face says he actually does mean to—"but we're on a tight timeline and need to boogie. If you'll just follow me, Hunter…"

"Give me a minute, Andy."

Huh. I never would have taken Glasses for an Andy. He's a little hipster I thought for sure he'd be an Atticus or something more original.

His eyes widen slightly. "It's just that we have to be downstairs in a matter of minutes and I want to make sure you have ample time to use the facilities if you need to."

"I'm fine," Hunter says firmly. "And they'll deal with me being a few minutes late."

Andy clenches his jaw and nods once before turning on his heel.

Hunter Sto—*Hunter*, doesn't seem the least bit

fazed by the conflict. "You have a theater blog?"

"Oh, um, it's a lot of things. Carrie, my friend who is engaged to <u>your </u>friend, Matthew, covers books and television. I focus on theater and movies. My roommate, Anna, is a musician so she's obviously the one to write all concerts and albums. Anything with the music scene."

"Do you have a lot of followers?"

"We're close to a hundred thousand and growing." I shrug like it's no big deal, even though it is a very big milestone to us. I keep suggesting a blog party. Carrie continues to shoot me down. She has no imagination.

Hunter whistles quietly. "That's not bad. Especially for a side gig."

"How do you know it's a side gig?" I feign offense, my palm resting on my chest.

The bright smile Hunter flashes is a contrast to the brooding personality he normally shows the public. I feel like I'm seeing a side of him reserved for people who are really in his life, not just popping through for an hour.

"You're a stage manager by trade. That passion doesn't just go away when your blog hits it big."

He's right. Only a fellow theater nerd would catch that, but only if he was paying attention to certain details. I can't believe he was paying attention.

"This may come off presumptuous of me, but I was wondering if you'd like to interview me for your blog."

I feel my eyes blink rapidly but I'm too stunned by his offer to care. An interview with him would put us on the map with online entertainment news. I can only imagine the number of new subscribers we would reach. And advertisers.

"I would be honored. Wow. Thank you."

He looks oddly relieved that I've accepted his offer. But how would my answer have been anything other than yes? There's no way this man has been turned down before.

Pulling his wallet out of his pocket, he snags a business card out and hands it to me. "This is my manager's information. He makes sure I'm where I'm supposed to be and when. Shoot him an email and he'll get it set up. Maybe tomorrow after the con but before I fly home?"

"That sounds perfect."

Popping his head into our space once again, Andy looks more flustered than ever. "I'm so sorry, but we really have to go. The boss is starting to freak out in my ear." Sure enough, Andy has an earpiece that seems to be attached to the walkie talkie at his hip. Old school, but effective I'm sure.

"He's right. Don't keep your fans waiting," I encourage, despite my own desire to stay here, talking to Hunter for as long as he'll let me.

Shoving his hands into his pockets, Hunter looks like he's preparing to put on a show again. Which means maybe this right here is the real Hunter Stone.

The man, not the actor, and certainly not the vampire cop. "Well, it was lovely getting to know you, Celeste."

"You too," I say and give a quick wave as he walks away, Andy rapid-firing bullet points of the next event.

"I have to say, I've volunteered at a lot of conventions," Klarissa says next to me, but my eyes are still glued to the now empty doorway. "But I have never seen an actor offer an interview or provide manager information."

"I'm as shocked as you are."

"Why don't you take a minute and email his manager before you forget. I've got a little time to set up for the next meet and greet."

Smiling gratefully at her, I take a seat at the table and let the last ten minutes of my life sink in. Then, I send a quick, yet professional email asking for an interview time for tomorrow, per Hunter's request.

Then I wait for a response.

It never comes.

Chapter 7

Hunter

I should apologize to the rest of the people in line. Their pictures are going to feature an insane looking version of me. Exhaustion explained how I felt this morning but now, it's straight fatigue. My back is tight and my jaw aches from the perma-grin I've had plastered on all day. It's the "actor" smile not the "me" smile. No, I've used that only twice today. Both times talking to Celeste.

Celeste.

It's been a long time since I've had an opportunity to talk theater with someone other than my mom. Even then, it's more about my days in the theater and not the craft itself. While Celeste and I didn't speak long, the time we were together was enough for me to note how her eyes danced at the topic. Her smile. Damn, she has a beautiful smile.

"Hunter, do you need anything?" Not *Toy Story* Andy asks while we have a short lull between attendees. It's the first free second I've had to grab a drink of water in close to two hours.

"A lobotomy," I mumble, rubbing my temples.

"What was that?"

Inhaling, I lift my lips to a small smile as I exhale. "Nothing. Do you think maybe they can turn the music down a little? The bass has somehow burrowed into the deep recesses of my brain."

"Like a worm?"

Chuckling, I nod my head and slap a hand on the kid's shoulder. "Yeah, man. Like a worm. If you could scale down the house music a little I may make it to the end of the line."

Stepping aside, Andy walks over to the photographer whose motto is the louder the music the better the pictures and leans in to speak in his ear. After a tense moment where Mr. Photog stiffens and pretends not to roll his eyes, the thumping music quiets a bit. It's not off, but it's quieter at least.

Hey, I get it. I'm an artist. We all have our own creative process. But it was about to make my brain explode. I need to remember to call Eddie, my manager, and tell him next con, no loud music in the tiny-ass rooms. Better to address that before an event to give everyone time to prepare themselves.

Taking a pull from the now room temperature bottle of water, I stretch my back and shake off the cobwebs in my head.

A scream rips through the room and I'm no longer sure which is worse—the shrieking or the music from hell.

"You're Hunter Stone. Ohmygosh!! I'm dying. I mean not like dying dying. Obviously, I'm still standing here and you—you're standing there. Holy crap on a cracker."

The young girl, maybe all of sixteen is rambling and hopping on her feet. She hasn't taken more than six steps toward me and the way she's bouncing on her heels, I don't know that she's going to. Rolling his eyes, the volunteer steps up next to her and gently nudges her forward.

Stumbling, she plasters on a huge smile. Her bright blue eyes widen.

"Ohmygosh. Oh. Hi. Um… I mean… this is the coolest thing ever."

"What's your name, sweetheart?"

I've heard Michael talk about women swooning and fainting at his feet. Until this moment, it isn't something I've experienced. Standing up straight, shoulders back, she plasters a shy smile on her face.

"Sarah. It's Sarah."

"Well, Sarah, how about we get that picture?"

Nodding, she steps next to me and I wrap my arm

around her shoulder, pulling her close. To my surprise, the rambling girl from a few minutes ago is gone and in her place is a teenage vixen. Turning so her front is nestled into my side, she tosses her head back, lifts her leg, and puckers her lips for the camera.

Well, okay then.

The look on Andy's face matches my thoughts as he chuckles and ushers Sarah out of the way. As she steps out, another woman is already posed and ready for her photo. It's a never-ending line of giggles, blushing women, and shy girls. The occasional man rolls through the line, a huge fan of the movie or someone who got a preview of the upcoming release.

Then a familiar face with bouncing blonde curls comes into view. Her bright smile is welcome. Familiar. Friendly. Beautiful.

"Hey you. Nice to see a familiar face," I say as she moves in closer. Celeste just smiles as she gets into position.

Opening my mouth to ask about our meeting tomorrow, I'm cut short by the photographer. "Okay, smile."

"So what time—?" she starts.

"Alright, thank you," Andy interrupts as he motions Celeste out of my space. She pauses only briefly, her mouth opening and closing as she's shuffled out the door.

A soft hand runs along my forearm pulling my attention back to the task at hand. An older woman, probably close to my grandmother's age flutters her long lashes my way. For the fourth time today, my smile is genuine as I settle her into my side.

After another hour of smiles, I'm finally released from my duties and head back to the green room to use the facilities and check my email for the location and time of my meeting with Celeste. Drying my hands with a paper towel, I open the door and step into the private room, tossing the wadded up paper into the trash. Some of my co-workers and event coordinators are meandering about and I nod my head in acknowledgement spotting the kid who kept me on track all weekend lingering.

Extending my hand in thanks, he greets me with a hearty shake. "Thank you for all you did this weekend. If you're around next year, hell if I'm around next year, I'm requesting you as my point person."

"I appreciate it, sir. It was a pleasure working with you. If my luck changes maybe I'll be here as a colleague next year."

"Oh, are you an actor?"

"Writer. I finished my first screenplay and have begun the query process."

Slipping a card from my wallet, I offer it to the kid. With a large grin, he takes it and smiles up at me. "If you want, send it to my agent. He'll get it to me and I'll take a look at it. I can't promise I'll be able to do much, but you never know."

His eyes are wide, not only at my offer but with

hope and determination. I remember those days. Early in my career, I was wide-eyed and earnest, looking for a break. Wishing for a break. Whether he sends the screenplay or not, just knowing someone is willing to take a chance on him may make all the difference as he works to break into the industry.

He nods his head before looking from me to the card and back again. Before he can make this more awkward, he's called away by someone with a clipboard and furrowed brow.

"Thanks again, Mr. Stone. Have a safe flight."

My flight. Pulling my phone from my pocket, I check the time. Four hours. I have hours until my flight leaves. It's enough time to meet Celeste and grab a bite to eat. Leaning against the wall, I check for new text messages from Eddie. Nothing. Maybe he just included me in the email confirmation with the Celeste.

Tapping the envelope icon, I scroll through my emails. This isn't my professional email; this is the personal one I use to communicate with Eddie and my non-celebrity life. Coupons, sales, and some Viagra should I need it. Good to know when the time comes. Hell, it's been so long since I've been with a woman, I may need it. Who even knows?

Running my hand through my hair, I scroll and scroll. Nothing from Eddie. It's unlikely he's in my spam folder but I check just the same. Again, nothing. I mean, there are more Viagra ads but no word from Eddie.

I should have gotten her number to set something up myself. I was playing it cool. Or at least attempting to by using my manager to set up the meeting. Cleary playing it cool is so not my strong suit. Maybe I should've tapped into my character Nikolai's persona. He may be a blood sucker, but the guy has moves. Not that I was going to put the moves on Celeste. We were going to grab a meal, talk theater, and maybe I'd remind myself why I started this life in the first place. Tap deep into my love of acting again.

Disappointed that she apparently didn't follow through, I push off the wall and move about the room, dropping my John Hancock on some last minute photos for the volunteers, and thanking everyone for a great event.

This weekend should have been my final commitment until we start table reads for the new season. Instead, I have months of promotion before the action film I snagged the lead role in releases. I knew taking on the part had the potential to launch me into a different caliber of stardom. What I hadn't counted on was how much the studio would invest in marketing the action flick and how interested they were in making me their new go-to leading man. That means interviews and photo shoots across the country. I'll be lucky to sleep in one hotel room two nights in a row.

What I need is downtime. A few months of letting my beard grow, not counting macros, and sleeping. It's been so long, I forget what it's like to curl up with my own pillow, in my own bed, and sleep until I wake because I'm rested instead of having to catch a flight. Moving down the hall, I stroll toward the private exit set up for the talent. When I approach security at the exit, I nod in acknowledgement as I'm shuffled into a waiting car.

As drained as I feel, one would think I've spent most of my life in the spotlight. The reality is, I've paid my dues, but my big break only happened a few years ago. Eddie warned me. He said the day would come that all the shitty parts and Ramen nights would pay off. What he failed to tell me was that I wouldn't have time to enjoy it.

I live a modest life. My home is nice but nothing extravagant. Taking care of my parents and providing for my younger siblings' education was never a second thought. The one indulgence I can claim is my fully loaded truck with a kick-ass sound system. Unlike many celebrities my age, I don't have a specially de-signed garage filled with sports cars.

Then there are the hotels. That's one area I don't skimp on and, thankfully, these conventions are usu-ally booked at the higher end chains which means, pri-vacy for the actors and my luggage waiting for me in my ride to the airport.

Pulling up Eddie's contact, I press the call button. Two rings. Three. Voicemail.

"Hey, it's Hunter. I'm just leaving the hotel. I was looking for an email from you about an interview… Anyway, give me a call when you have a chance."

I end the call and settle back into the plush leather. The buildings are a blur as the car maneuvers through downtown Chicago. Glancing at the console, I note the time. Not that the minutes are moving quickly. The least the city could do is offer a little traffic to make the drive to the airport longer. Give me a little more time before I have to be "on" again.

Still, no call from Eddie. I fire off a message regarding my early arrival at the airport, so the TSA escort is ready for me. I don't expect to be mobbed by paparazzi or fans like some, but I've learned to never assume.

Yawning, I lean my head back and close my eyes. In just a few hours I'll be home and able to block out the world for a few days. Catch up on some rest and plan a trip to see my family. I could use some of my mama's home cooking and uncle time with my nieces and nephews.

I startle when the door opens, pulling me from my dream-like state. Unfolding myself out the car, I rise to my full height and put on a smile. When I turn to thank the driver, he's already rounded the car and is settling behind his seat. Well, okay then.

"Sir, if you're ready?" The TSA agent asks. This guy is huge and pushing the sleeves of his shirt to its limits.

"Sure…"

"Joe."

"Lead the way, Joe."

Following my guide, I keep a light smile on my face and my gaze low and ahead as we weave through the crowd and to the special security lane. Not all airports offer this luxury and while it makes me uncomfortable to be singled out, I can't imagine the level of anxiety I'd feel or how much of a distraction it could be to be one of the hundreds in the regular security line.

Once my backpack and I are both scanned, I slip my earbuds in and resume listening to the classic rock playlist I had on this morning. Double checking the app on my phone, I confirm I need to walk to the far end of this terminal for the airline's private lounge. So far I haven't been noticed, and I hope to keep it that way until I make it to the elevator, which will drop me in the lobby of the lounge.

A small child darts in front of me and I stop short of running her over. The mother offers me a small smile before stumbling. So much for going unrecognized. On instinct, I reach down to help the woman, my earbud slipping from my ear. Catching it before it hits the ground, I slip it in my pocket.

"You're… Ohmygosh…" Before she can say another word, the little girl screeches in the distance. Abandoning me, the woman rushes to her child.

Picking up the pace, I rush to the sign identifying the lounge elevators. By some miracle, they open, and a woman steps out, pulling a suitcase behind her. Slipping between the doors, I push the close button just as I hear my name again.

Adjusting my backpack on my shoulder, I pull the

rogue earbud from my pocket. Just as I set it to my ear, I hear my name in the distance. Shit.

Chapter 8

Celeste

When I booked my flight home, I thought leaving before the convention was officially over would be fine. As long as I got my picture, my autograph and my round table discussion with Hunter Stone, I would be sitting on Cloud Nine without a care in the world.

I was wrong. I'm sitting in an airport chair with a rip in the upholstery that keeps pinching my leg and lamenting the fact that I am missing the closing ceremony simply so I can catch the cheapest flight home. Not that I had much of a choice. I used almost all my points on the hotel for Carrie's wedding which meant my options for cheap flights were more limited. Still, I feel like something amazing is going to happen back at the hotel when I'm not there. Which is likely given my track record with even getting to the con in the first place.

Who knew that I, Celeste Pumperkin, hater of all things vampire except Hunter Stone's artistic interpretation, would become a fangirl over a TV show about paranormal crime fighters? But after spending three days immersed in the Prince of Darkness fandom, I get it now. And I'm almost ashamed to admit I might try that vampire series Carrie has been pressuring me to read for several years now. It helps that I can visualize Hunter Stone in the lead role of that series. No one has to know that part except me.

Opening up my email again, I blow out an exaggerated sigh. Still no response from this Eddie guy who allegedly manages Hunter's schedule. I've triple checked that I sent my email request to the correct address and I have made sure it isn't stuck in my drafts. I don't understand why I wouldn't get a response. Not even a "Buzz off stalker, he was kidding." or something equally humiliating. The whole thing depresses me, which is ridiculous. I did everything I came here for. That moment, where Hunter offered me an interview, was just an additional memory no one else in the world has. That's what I need to focus on, not the disappointment of no follow-through.

I sigh again and push my phone back down into my crossbody purse and glance down at my laptop. There are still forty-five minutes until we start the boarding process so I could work on my screenplay. If only the words would come. I still can't figure out why the story is so vivid in my brain but when I start writing, it turns into unorganized, unreadable crap.

Maybe now isn't the time to try and be creative. My mind is still reeling with images of this weekend so I might as well begin uploading pictures for the blog post I'll be doing about the convention. While the focus of the weekend was primarily the television show, Carrie's forte, the tie-in to the upcoming movie makes it easy enough for me to report on. Besides, it's an event people would love to see on our page regardless of which one of us attended.

I tap my fingers against the keys, but don't actually depress them as the creative juices in my head begin to flow. The hum of the airport with its squawky overhead announcements and people racing back and forth make an oddly calming background noise. Chaos is my calm. Strange as that sounds.

Just as my thoughts begin to settle and the words put themselves in the right order, unexpected movement in my peripheral vision distracts me. Looking over, it appears a child has darted out into foot traffic causing some sort of collision. The women who I assume is the mother is frozen in front of a man who looks an awful lot like the one I've been trying to track down, although he's clearly incognito.

"You're… ohmygosh…" she says before darting after her screeching child who is still running.

Holy crap. Now is my chance.

"Hunter!" I yell, feeling bad to call him out in public like this, but not wanting to miss him again either.

He doesn't stop, in fact his pace seems to pick up.

Closing my laptop and shoving it into my bag, I move as quickly as I can, which is about as quick as a salmon swimming upstream. Fortunately, I only have my electronics bag and my purse, but unfortunately, the zippers on both seem to have stopped working at this exact moment. I race after him, trying to juggle everything without dropping my water bottle and phone.

"Hunter!" I call again just as the elevator door he disappeared into closes.

I come to my own screeching halt when I notice it's one of the airline's VIP lounges. I'm not sure how to proceed. I don't fly often, but when I do, I take the cheapest route, my only goal to get from Point A to Point B safely. I don't need the extra frills. But that also means I've never been inside a VIP lounge before. Well, except for the one this past weekend at the hotel. I wonder if they're the same.

One thing is for sure—I need to get in there, even if it is only to have Hunter tell me he changed his mind and doesn't want to be interviewed anymore. That I can deal with. What I can't deal with is this "in limbo" feeling.

Balancing as my bag slides off my shoulder and down my arm, I do a quick search on my phone about who can use a VIP lounge in an airport and how. And wouldn't you know it, my freaking Wi-Fi isn't connecting.

Making a spontaneous decision, I decide to go for it, so I push the up button and wait. And wait. Wow, for luxury this thing isn't in much of a hurry. When the chrome doors open, I exhale in relief that it is empty and not manned by a stern security guard. The whoosh of the elevator causes me to stumble where I stand, clutching my bag and electronics to my chest. As quickly as it took off, it stops and the doors open.

With a deep breath, I exit and step into a bright foyer. A large reception desk with three uniformed women fills one side of the space while the other is a large mirror. People meander around in the distance. Some on their phones, others carrying drinks and food in their hands. My stomach takes that moment to grumble. Maybe I can kill two birds with one stone. Food and an interview.

Shaking off the cobwebs in my head as I take in the opulence of the room, my shoulder is hit by a man wearing some sort of uniform. I don't know his role here, whatever it is, but the job must not include apologizing for our near accident. He doesn't say anything. Instead he gives me the once over, clearly assessing my threat level. I'm unclear what, exactly, I'm a potential threat to, but I don't make any sudden movements while he looks at me. I don't really have time to be tackled to the ground and stuck in a windowless room while security decides if I can get on the plane home.

Eventually, I see a small shrug and he turns away from me, never saying a word. Just leaves.

That was weird, but not entirely unexpected for how my life goes when it comes to a convention weekend. Four years' worth of the universe playing with me is not easily written off as coincidence.

As I step farther into the foyer, I right my scattered mess and suck in a deep breath, calming my nerves and racing heart. The woman at the desk greets me with an immediate smile.

"Hello. How can I help you today?" She's tall and blonde with her hair pulled back in a perfect chignon and dressed in an outfit that reminds me of a Pan Am stewardess circa the 1950s. She's very glam. If that's any indication of how the lounge is run, I'm a fan already.

Flashing her a kind smile I step up to the counter. "I'm not a Premiere member but I'd like to see about using the lounge for the day." And by day I mean the next half hour before my flight begins boarding.

"Absolutely," she replies. "We have some availability at the moment and our dinner buffet was just put out for your enjoyment."

"Wonderful," I say demurely even though I kind of want to clap my hands together at the thought of a fancy meal. Maybe I need to become a Premiere member after all for perks like this.

"I'll just need a photo ID and your boarding pass please."

Finding my driver's license is easy and I hand it over quickly. My boarding pass, on the other hand, seems to be hiding from me. I'm not surprised. I shoved everything in my bag when I was racing after Hunter. It probably got smooshed at the bottom. This is why I hate disorganization. It's so much faster and easier when things are in their proper places.

A few clicks of her keyboard while I search for my ticket and she "hmms." "I'm not finding you in our system, Miss Pump…er…Pumperkin. I'll have to search it by your itinerary number."

Feeling a little flustered from this mess, I blow a wayward curl out of my face. "I'm so sorry. I'm usually more organized than this." *Unless I'm chasing after movie stars…* "Give me one second. It's my first time using the lounge."

"Take your time." Her words are very polite, but I notice a tinge of unhappiness at me being frazzled. I suppose those who use the lounge regularly are probably better prepared than I am to check in.

It takes a few more minutes and practically emptying out my bag all over the floor to remember what I'm looking for is actually in my purse. Sounds about right for my day.

"Sorry about that," I say sheepishly as I hand it over. "I put it in my purse so I wouldn't lose it. Typical, right?"

She is not amused. Even less so when she looks at my boarding pass.

"Ma'am, you're not flying our airline."

"Does that make a difference?"

"The VIP lounges are airline specific." Sliding my boarding pass across the counter, her friendly demeanor practically evaporates. "And unfortunately, the *discount* airline you're flying doesn't have one in this airport. Or anywhere."

She says the word "discount" like it's offensive to her. I guess she's never had to decide between upgrading to an airline that provides a drink and peanuts and paying the electric bill. Lucky her.

"So then why can't I use this one? I'm willing to pay like everyone else."

"That's not the way it works. Only our customers can use our lounges."

This can't be happening. I need in that lounge. I need to get my interview with Hunter while I'm… err, *it's* still fresh in his mind. Once he hits the next convention or press junket or wherever he's going next, I'll be a forgotten memory.

I know this poor woman's hands are tied, but maybe I can appeal to her success as a professional.

Leaning forward, a huge smile on my face I say, "I understand what you're saying." Her shoulders relax at my non-threatening tone. "But Hunter Stone just walked in there."

Her spine straightens once again, and I realize too late I've made a mistake dropping his name.

"No! No, I'm not a fan," I try to backtrack. "I mean I am, because who isn't? I actually know him from years ago when he was working well off-Broadway."

Stop babbling, Celeste. Get to the point.

Chuckling lightly, I wave my hand. "You don't

care about that. My point is, I'm a blogger."

Wrong again. Now she looks like she's about to call that giant "stare me down without a word" guy back. He can't have gotten far so I better fix this.

"Hunter and I are both leaving a convention where we spoke multiple times." I begin digging around my bag for evidence. "He offered to let me interview him before he left and gave me this card, see?"

I hand her the business card as proof. She looks down at it and frowns. "This says Eddie Addison on it."

"Right. That's his manager. I emailed him but haven't heard back and this would be a great time to knock out the interview so we can both go on our way."

"Ms. Pumpernickle…"

"Pumperkin…"

"Are you suggesting I ignore the fact that you aren't a member here, aren't even a customer of our airline, so you, as a member of the press, can harass one of our celebrity clients?"

"No! Oh gosh no! We're actually sort of friends—ish. He's friends with Matthew Roberts, who is marrying my best friend, Carrie Myers. You can look it up online. There was a small magazine spread about it. Oh! I know!" The dig in my purse begins once again. Why can't I find anything in here? I know why… receipts. I have all of them from this weekend for tax purposes, making my usually organized purse a mess. Figures.

Finally I find what I'm looking for. "Here, see?" I hand her yet another business card. "This is our blog and website. We cover books and movies and… anyway, you can see my name right there and Carrie's is right above mine. You know to cross reference that I know Matthew and therefore Hunter…"

Even as the words come out of my mouth, I know how weak my argument is. I might as well say I know Kevin Bacon because there's only six degrees of separation.

"This card says the website is owned by Celestial Starr and Carrie Mibooks."

"Those are our blog names… for… privacy reasons."

I squeeze my eyes shut, not even having to look at her to know this conversation is over. My face is flaming with the humiliation I'm feeling. Quietly, I begin repacking all my belongings, careful to get everything in the correct places so I don't have to re-organize again later.

When I'm finally situated, I take my boarding pass off the counter.

"I'm sorry to have wasted your time."

Turning toward the door, she stops me.

"Ms. Pumpernickle…"

I don't bother correcting her, feeling a tiny bit of hope that she's changed her mind and will have pity on me.

"I don't need these business cards."

She reaches her arm out, holding the cards with two fingers like they'll infect her with whatever has me acting a fool.

Sheepishly, I take them from her and exit the reception area as quickly as I can, relieved the windows are frosted and no one in the concourse was able to witness my humiliation.

Chapter 9

Hunter

Two months later

It may not be a flight home to my bed and much missed pillow but I'm not complaining. A long weekend in Turks and Caicos may be exactly what I need. To say I was surprised when I received an invitation to Matthew Roberts's wedding would be an understatement. Sure, we've gotten to know each other better over the last few months, having hung out a few times when our paths have crossed for work. But I always assumed destination weddings were for close family and friends.

Yet, here I am, raising my seat to its upright position as we make our descent over the pristine azure water. This weekend will hopefully be a far cry from the last vacation I took. That weekend of camping with my family left me with a body covered in mosquito bites and a kink in my neck that took days to work out. Of course, I was seventeen and shared a tent with my brother, but that's neither here nor there.

Come to think of it, it's been more than a decade since I have had any sort of vacation. While attending a wedding doesn't exactly scream "vacation," an opportunity to spend a few days at a tropical resort was the selling point.

Settling in, the flight attendant catches my eye as she peers from her seat in the galley. She's pretty with dark brown hair pulled back in a tight bun, blunt bangs framing her big brown eyes. I have no doubt if I flashed a megawatt smile, she would be putty in my hands. The same hands that would be filled with her body. But, that's not my style. I don't hook up with random women even if it's been longer than I'm willing to admit to myself since I've been with anyone. The potential consequences aren't worth it at this stage of my career. One picture of my naked ass in the tabloids and my burgeoning career could be over before it has really started.

As the wheels touch down and my fellow passengers and I bounce in our seat, I can feel the tension of the past six months lessen. My muscles are pulled tight, but I have no doubt by the end of the weekend, I'll at least be able to breathe easier.

I half expected Eddie to convince me to cancel this trip. While our U.S. promotional tour for the blockbuster was relatively standard, the European portion was nothing but delays and rescheduling. Add in a nasty flu bug that made its way through the circuit and the reshoots for Prince of Darkness and I'm wiped. Of course, there's no rest for the weary and one day in the future I'll look back at this time as some of the best in my life.

At least that's what I'm told. I think those people are high or delusional.

When the captain signals we can unfasten our seatbelts and prepare to deplane, I pull my phone from where it's been nestled in the pocket of the seat in front of me and switch it off airplane mode. I immediately have regrets as notification upon notification come through. Without another thought, I shoot a quick message to my mom letting her know I arrived and then quickly power it down. It's unlike me to go off the grid, to allow myself time to relax. But I promised myself I would take this weekend to reset my internal battery.

Rising from my seat, I stretch my back and gather my things before sliding on my sunglasses and filing out of the plane. A quick thank you to the crew and I step onto the jetway, the smell of saltwater fills my senses. I've always liked the beach, but it's been years since I've had the downtime to really enjoy it. Maybe that's been part of my problem. I've sacrificed the things I've enjoyed in life, forgotten why I started this career in the first place, to get where I am but at what cost? I'm closing in on thirty years old and have the success I've dreamed of, but my sense of balance is non-existent. There's no one to share all of this with.

Moving around baggage claim is seamless. Unlike

airports in the states, nobody seems to care that I'm standing among them. It helps that I haven't shaved in a week, let my hair grow longer, and am wearing sunglasses indoors. Makes me harder to recognize. Not that anyone is paying attention. Couples cuddle and children dance around, pure joy expressed in their smiles and laughs. Here I stand, a lone man with a backpack. That's depressing.

A woman next to me struggles with her suitcase so I step up and help her, grabbing the handle and lugging it off the conveyor belt. Dang, what does she have in here? A body?

"Thank you," she says with a smile.

"You're welcome."

"Have a nice trip." With that statement she shuffles away, pulling her luggage beside her. Huh. No recognition. Looks like my vacation persona is working. I'm not sure if I should be relieved or slightly offended.

Once I've secured my own suitcase, I scan the space for the exit and spot a man holding a sign with "Stone" printed on it. Nodding in recognition, I approach the gentleman.

"Mr. Stone?"

"That's me."

"Right this way, sir. I'll take your luggage."

Passing off the suitcase, I follow him out into the bright sunlight. The upside to an overnight flight is arriving midday when the sun is high in the sky. The ocean breeze is welcome as we make our way to the waiting town car. Sliding into the back seat, I instinctively reach for my phone but remember it is powered off. I'm leaving it that way. I will enjoy the down time and my first real vacation.

Instead, I open the window and take in the scenery before me, willing my mind and body to calm and embrace the next few days of relaxation. Celebration of a friend and his future. It isn't a long drive to the resort and when we arrive I'm pleasantly surprised to see the hotel resembles a large southern estate more than a traditional hotel.

Again, nobody seems to give me a second look as I check in. The staff is polite but also unfazed by my presence and for the first time in a long time, I feel like my old self not the actor Hunter Stone. Following the bell captain to my room, I realize I am still wearing my sunglasses. Well if that doesn't scream "douchebag" I don't know what does. Sunglasses indoors. *Way to be a stereotype, Hunter.*

Stepping into the room, I'm taken aback by its opulence. Two rooms separated by a pair of French doors, the bright white furniture and blue walls feel like the space is actually an extension of the outdoors more than anything.

"Your private veranda is just there, sir. I believe the wedding party has provided an itinerary with your welcome basket."

Turning my attention to the kind man, I smile and reach for my wallet pulling a twenty out and placing it in his palm. Nodding, he thanks me and exits the room. With a deep inhale and exhale, exhaustion takes over once again.

Moving to the large basket of snacks and champagne, I lift the card clearly setting out the itinerary of the weekend. I've already missed the welcome brunch and water sports are in full effect according to this schedule. Tonight is a cocktail hour and dinner for all guests before an "early to bed" note since tomorrow is the wedding day. Looking at the time, I note I have just about three hours until the cocktail portion of the evening begins.

Just enough time for a nap and a shower. I walk over to the French doors leading to the private veranda the man pointed out. The view is breathtaking. White sandy beaches as far as the eye can see with that pristine water I saw from the plane stretched out in front of me.

The energy I've held onto slowly dissipates and I turn toward the bedroom, stripping off my clothes as I go. Once I'm in only my boxer briefs, I slip between the covers and realize I should set an alarm. That would involve turning my phone on. Instead, I reach for the phone on the side table and call the front desk for a wakeup call.

It isn't long before the crashing waves lull me to a much needed sleep.

As I lift the tumbler of amber liquid to my lips, I scan the party. A few faces I recognize from work—mostly photographers and models. I met Matthew on a photo shoot, so it's expected to see industry people here but what I notice most of all is that everyone appears to be well acquainted. Their body language is relaxed and intimate like they are all family and close friends. Here I stand, the lone wolf. An awkward lone wolf because I haven't moved from this bar since I arrived.

The nap earlier was exactly what I needed but it was also only a drop in the bucket for the amount of rest I need. I'm burning the candle at more than one end if that's even possible. A hand grips my shoulder, pulling my attention from people watching.

"Hey man, good to see you. Thanks for coming."

My lips lift to a real smile as I turn to face the groom. Standing beside him is a beautiful woman in a floor length blue dress. Her smile is wide and her eyes full of happiness.

"You must be Carrie. It's nice to finally meet you. Thank you for having me."

"No, thank you for being here. I was beginning to wonder if this guy was full of it and making up your friendship."

Her wink makes me laugh as she wraps me in a tight hug. When we separate, I extend my hand to Matthew who shakes it before pulling me into a man-hug with a smack on the back.

"How was your flight? Is your room okay?" Matthew asks, as he accepts a drink from his bride-to-be.

"Everything has been great. I'm sorry I couldn't get here yesterday with everyone. My schedule is crazy right now."

"No worries, man. We knew you were coming straight from Europe. We're just happy to have you here."

Before either of us can say anything, a little girl wearing a crown approaches us, skipping the entire way. At first glance, I'd assume she's already dressed for tomorrow's wedding by the sparkly pink dress she's wearing. Then I recognize it as a dress-up outfit. One of my nieces has the same one, courtesy of her favorite uncle—me.

"Daddy, when is the dancing? I am so ready!"

Laughing, he looks down at her with love in his eyes and smiles. "Sprite, I told you the dancing is tomorrow after the wedding. This is just to spend time with our guests. Say hello to Mr. Stone."

Calypso, lovingly referred to as Sprite by her family, groans and she throws her head back, hand to her forehead before turning her attention my way. Looks like Matthew may have a little actress on his hands.

"Hi," the little one grumbles.

"Hello there. I like your dress. It's very pretty."

The compliment seems to do the trick and her face lights up as she spins in a circle. "Thanks. It's not better than Elsa's blue one. But I left that one at home because it's Luke's favorite."

I recognize the name as characters from a movie my sister complains about watching on a constant loop. Before I can comment further, the blushing bride takes over.

"Okay little princess, let's go mingle. It was nice to meet you, Hunter." Carrie takes the little girl's hand and they walk away, chattering the entire time.

It's then that I see a mess of curls across the pool. It couldn't be. Well, I mean it could be since we share mutual friends, but I'm surprised, nonetheless. It never occurred to me that I would see Celeste again after my botched attempt to spend some time with her. Yet, there she is. I watch her move around, laughing and talking as she makes her way through the crowd.

"I need to follow my future wife's lead and work the crowd before the wedding planner gives me the side eye again," Matthew interjects, completely unaware I forgot he was standing next to me. "I swear, she's worse than Donna on a photo shoot. Who knew someone helping you with the happiest day of your life could be more of a task maker than a Type A romance author?"

Once again, I have no idea who he's talking about. Maybe I need to leave my post and make some conversation with the other guests. "Don't worry about me. Go do your groom thing."

Nodding his head, he walks away. For the next few hours, I sip on my whiskey and accept hors d'oeuvres from waiters as they pass by. Ignoring my own advice to socialize, I never move from this side of the pool. Actually, I've stayed close to this pillar and kept myself hidden from the rest of the group. Not that I'm hiding per se, I just like watching Celeste. The way she throws her head back in full belly laughs. Her hair bouncing around carefree with every movement.

Celeste is carefree and I envy that part of her.

"For God's sake, would you just go talk to her?" Matthew's voice startles me and I jump, turning to face him. I can feel the heat on my skin in embarrassment. Busted.

"Uh, who?"

"Celeste. You've been stalking her all night."

"No I haven't. And don't you have other more pressing matters to attend to than what I'm doing?"

"Dude. It's hard to ignore the fact that you haven't moved all night. You look like a creeper. A lumberjack creeper with that beard you've got. By the way, my fiancé has asked me if I'll grow one. So thanks for that." He claps his hand on my shoulder. "If you like her so much, go talk to her."

"I… no… that would be awkward." Especially since she rejected my offer the last time we spoke.

"Would it? I have listened to Celeste and my wife discuss this Prince of Darkness convention and all things Hunter Stone for a year. A year! Celeste has been crushing on you way longer than that."

"On me?"

That makes no sense. If she was so interested, why didn't she send Eddie an email? I know him well enough to know he didn't get a request from her. Eddie's always looking for ways to reach a new demographic. He would have jumped all over the chance to capture a hundred thousand potential fans.

"Hell yeah. It all has something to do with an off-off-Broadway show or something. I don't even know."

"Oh." That makes sense. She was really excited about the playbill. Something we had in common. "So I should talk to her?"

"Uh, yeah."

"What if she decides she doesn't like me?"

"What if she does?"

Abandoning me and our conversation, Matthew leaves me to speak with someone who is calling his name and waving his arm above his head. Everyone here is very animated. I stand here for another beat and consider what he's said. I've already met her so it isn't like it would be awkward to say hello, would it?

We spoke for what probably only amounted to ten complete minutes of conversation over the course of a weekend. Once. It isn't as if we even exchanged numbers.

But do I do as my friend suggested? Walk across this party and start a conversation with the only woman who has held my interest in longer than I'd care to admit?

Nope. At least not tonight. I take my whiskey and go to my room. Alone.

Chapter 10

Celeste

"**I** now pronounce you husband and wife. You may kiss the bride."

Cheers and catcalls erupt from the small crowd as Matthew and Carrie make out like a couple of horny teenagers on prom night, completely oblivious to the world around them. Or maybe they just don't care. They're officially married now. Who's going to stop him from sticking his tongue down her throat?

"Dad. *Daddy*, gross." Calypso, Matthew's spunky and hilarious daughter tugs on his sleeve, looking over her shoulder to see the reaction of the guests. The look on her face screams "Do you people see this? Make them stop!" She looks horrified. "Dad!"

The happy couple framed by the bamboo pergola adorned with flowing white fabric and flowers finally separates, smiling at each other before turning toward the crowd. As Matthew raises their clasped hands in victory, the officiant announces, "Ladies and gentlemen, I present to you, Mr. and Mrs. Roberts and family."

Another round of cheers serenade the trio as they stroll down the makeshift aisle toward the pool area where the reception will be held.

It was important to Matthew and Carrie that the wedding be about their new family, so they skipped the usual wedding party, keeping it to only themselves and Calypso. While the family meets with the photographer for pictures, the guests all head straight for the open bar. I'll have to thank Matthew for this gift later.

As I step up to the bar, I twist my lips in contemplation. I'm in the mood for something a little sweeter to go with the ambiance of a tropical vacation. "Do you happen to have sangria?" I ask the bartender, who nods his response. Come to think of it, maybe I should have a piña colada. It's not every day I'm at a wedding on the beach, enjoying perfect temperatures and the sounds of waves in the background.

Too late. My drink is handed to me as a guy approaches to my left. Not behind me in line like a civilized person. Doesn't this guy know how open bars work? We all get a drink. His elbows rest on the small bar top, almost bumping into me. Great. The reception hasn't even begun and I'm already about to be hit on. I'm all for a little flirt session and can't say I would be opposed to a one-night stand. But at a wedding? So cliché.

"Don't I know you?"

Worst. Line. Ever.

I drop a bill in the tip jar and wonder why men can't be more creative. Is the art of the pick-up line dead? Taking a sip of the deliciousness that is my sangria, I wait a beat before responding, never turning to face the guy. "You'll have to do better than that."

"What?"

"You know, your pick-up line. Try again." I turn to the poor sucker and wait for something more interesting to come out of his mouth while I sip more of my drink. Tasty. Maybe this was the right choice of drink for the night.

"No, really. I know you." I keep my eye roll at bay. Yes, I'm disappointed by his lack of imagination but since he is likely one of Matthew's friends, I still want to be polite. I let him finish his latest effort. "You're Celeste. We met at the Prince of Darkness con. You're a blogger of all things theater and were supposed to email my manager for an interview but never did. And I have had a couple of shots of whiskey, enough to loosen my tongue to say I was disappointed you didn't follow through."

My jaw drops open as I take in his appearance. There is no way Hunter Stone is standing in front of me. He looks so different than the last time I saw him. The transformation from vampire cop to tourist is incredible.

"Wait… Hunter?" I know I sound completely confused, but I am. I knew he was friends with Matthew, but I had no idea they were close enough for him to be at the wedding. I make a mental note to berate Carrie for this lack of information. Speaking of, I quickly scan the crowd, spotting Calypso and the grandparents. Suspiciously, the bride and groom are nowhere in sight. I don't even want to know why.

"You, but…" I shake my head as I try to wrap my brain around this turn of events. "You have a beard. And your hair is long. And wavy. Holy shit, you look totally different. Actually, you kind of look like a lumberjack."

He chuckles, and based on that sound, there is no denying the man who has starred in most—okay all—of my fantasies over the last few months is well and truly standing in front of me.

Shoving his hands in his dark blue pants pockets, he smiles shyly. "I've been hearing that a lot lately. I was trying to blend in. I guess it worked."

"I'll say." This version of Hunter Stone is unexpected but not unwelcome. A quick perusal of him from head to toe sends a shiver up my spine. The navy pants look to be tailored perfectly to his body and the white button-down shirt is fitted but not too tight. The collar is open, showing off his olive skin, but it's the rolled up sleeves that show off his forearms that have me taking a hearty sip of my drink. And then it hits me. "And what do you mean I never emailed? I did it that day." Yes, I'm trying to be polite, but I'm still a bit miffed the offer was extended and then taken back with no explanation.

Actually, I'm not really irritated anymore. I'd moved on from the incident after a couple weeks of being home so I'm not really sure why I am suddenly on the defense. I blame the bottle, okay bottles, of champagne Carrie and I consumed in her suite before the ceremony. Maybe Hunter isn't the only one with loose lips right now.

"What are you talking about?" His brows furrow together. "I had Eddie checking for your email for two weeks. You never sent him one."

"Well he didn't check it then because I sent it before I even left that room. Ask the volunteer. She made me sit down and do it right then so I wouldn't forget."

Hunter opens his mouth to reply but changes his mind, pushing his hair back instead. "I don't understand. Why would Eddie not schedule an interview? He's a media whore. That doesn't make any sense."

I watch as the frustration and confusion play out on his face. Hunter seems genuinely concerned about this snafu. Maybe even wondering if Eddie betrayed him and if so, why. The strong, alpha persona he plays on TV is gone, replaced by a sensitive, empathetic man. This isn't "Hunter Stone" standing in front of me. This is the real Hunter.

"I'm so sorry, Celeste. I hope the scheduling issue didn't mess anything up with your blog."

"It was fine. Don't worry about that." His features

relax a bit. "Sure I was disappointed, but things happen, you know? If you only knew how many years I was supposed to go to before I finally made it, you'd know this was par for the course."

Understatement of the year, even if he doesn't know it.

"I'd like to make it up to you. Do you maybe want to do the interview now?"

"During the wedding reception?"

He shrugs. Something about it tells me he really doesn't want to. And that's when I see it. I've been so focused on his hair and his beard, I didn't notice the circles under his eyes until now. The man is exhausted. This is probably the only vacation he's had in way too long. As much as I want that interview, now isn't the time.

Putting my hand on his forearm, I swear his skin burns my hand. It's like a zap of electricity. More than likely, it's the tiny hairs on his arm being extra hot from a tropical sun, but I still notice. "We're in Turks and Caicos. I'm deeming it a no-work zone. How about we find a table and just talk like friends instead?"

His mega-watt smile, the same one I saw after everyone else had left our meet and greet flashes my way. "I'd like that."

"Do you want to order a drink while we're here?"

Nodding, he places an order for a whiskey on the rocks and a water. I suck down the rest of my sangria and order another. With our drinks in hand, we wind our way through the outdoor space, passing the newly-weds who have reappeared and are speaking to the DJ before he asks everyone to take their seats as the bride and groom move to the middle of the small dance floor area. A sweet love song fills the air as the happy couple sways together. I ignore the fact that Carrie looks a little more disheveled than she did thirty minutes ago. None of my business and the less I know the better. Besides, who can blame her? Her husband is hot.

But so is the guy walking close behind me. Even with No-Shave-Vacation, which apparently also means not keeping the new beard cleaned up, he's still incredibly attractive, his piercing green eyes only one-upped by the magnificent smile he gives me. When we sit, I also notice his teeth fidgeting with his bottom lip. Is it a nervous tell? Interesting.

"Is this your first time in Turks and Caicos?"

"It is," he says, stretching his long legs out in front of him. His feet cross at the ankles and I find it incredibly sexy, which is the weirdest thought I've had all day. "I realized yesterday this is my first vacation in over a decade."

No wonder he looks this exhausted. "What? That's too long."

"I know," he says with an amused grin. "But you know how it is. Once I moved to New York, it was all about my career. I was living off Ramen and picking up quarters on the sidewalk, hoping to collect enough for rent. A vacation was a distant fantasy."

I neglect to tell him that's how I still live.

"Then once I joined the cast, work has been non-stop. I travel quite often but don't actually stop to enjoy it. I'm glad I'm finally getting to breathe for a few days. Plus it beats the hell out of camping with my brother."

"Was that your last vacation?" I settle back in my chair, enjoying the warm breeze blowing through my hair.

"Yep. The whole family went. My dad had us convinced it would be a fun family outing."

"Uh oh. Sounds like there's a story there," I say as I bring my drink to my lips.

The sound of his quiet laughter is something I could get used to. "Let's just say we discovered quickly my mother is more of a glamper than a camper."

"I agree with her on that one. So your parents are still together?"

"Going on thirty-five years."

"Wow. That's impressive. I think my parents maybe lasted five before calling it quits."

Hunter's eyes soften, like every other person who finds out my parents are divorced. "I'm so sorry. That must have been hard."

I shrug. "Not really. I was little so it's my normal. Besides, two houses means double everything… holidays, presents, grandparents. Worked to my benefit."

"That doesn't sound bad at all."

"It wasn't. And since my mother loves to travel and it was just the two of us, we spent a lot of time exploring. She's in the Galapagos Islands with her husband now."

We continue talking about anything and everything, as the evening turns into night: his European tour that sounds like a total shit show, my inability to make it to a convention for three years running which he found way too humorous, the role he hopes to get in a small Sundance type film, my disappointment at being passed over for a second assistant stage manager position on a Broadway show.

We laugh. We talk serious. We share secrets. And we drink. Lord, do we drink. The sangria and whiskey he's having never stop flowing and before I know it, we're wrapped in each other's arms on the dance floor, slow dancing to a fast song, not caring at all that Matthew has made more than one quip about our "new-found romance" as he calls it. That man needs to quit reading the books he's on the cover of.

Hunter and I aren't as blitzed as our friends seem to think. We're not propped up on each other. No, we're just embracing. I'll be damned if it doesn't feel better than I imagined it would. So it's not the alcohol fueling this moment. It's genuine, true attraction.

I've always heard it's a bad idea to meet your celebrity crush because when they turn out to be completely different than you expected, it ruins the whole fantasy for you. In Hunter's case, that's true. He is not at all who his persona is—he's better. He's genuine and kind, funny and easygoing. And he doesn't have a cocky bone in his body. Quite the contrary. He's actually quite reserved. Almost shy. All of the traits I love about a man wrapped up in a beautiful package. It's almost jarring how much we click. But we do, in so many ways.

Underneath the light of paper lanterns and tiki torches, his large hand rests on my lower back, holding me close, the other hand grips mine on his chest as we sway. Cheek to cheek, his nose brushes against my temple every once in a while. My skin is peppered with goose bumps. I could blame the ocean breeze, but I won't. It's all Hunter Stone. When he leans down to press a kiss to my neck, my entire body lights up. This isn't just a man on vacation. This is a man feeling the same attraction I am. A man who wants me as much as I want him. And I'm not going to let Hunter slip away from me again.

Reaching up, I quietly speak in his ear. "Would it be presumptuous of me to ask if you'd like to come back to my room?"

He pulls back to really look at me, a startled expression gracing his beautiful face. "Are you sure?"

I nod. "I wouldn't normally ask after meeting someone a few hours ago. But we met before. Several times. Well, it was all in one day, but it didn't feel like it."

He chuckles. "I get it. Each one of those events felt like they were a day long."

"For you they practically were. My point is, I don't want us to miss the opportunity. While we're in this vacation bubble, no stress from the outside world."

I can't ignore the deep breath he takes, but then he smiles. "I don't think anything could make me happier in this moment than going back to your room with you."

This time, I'm the one biting my bottom lip nervously. Looking around, I know no one is paying attention to us.

"Come on," I say and grab his hand, leading him across the dance floor and through the courtyard to my room.

We race to the elevator to take us to the fourth floor where my room is. It takes far too long for the lift to arrive, probably because of the family of five who has twice as many bags trying to get off on the first floor where we're waiting. But we finally get on and the doors close.

The energy is palpable between us. Sexual tension rolls off both of us in waves. When he stands behind me and softly runs his fingers down my arms, goose bumps break out across my whole body and I practically melt into the floor. This isn't even foreplay and I'm already about to explode. If that's any indication, this is going to be a very good night.

The doors open revealing a hallway void of anyone else. Within seconds, we're standing at my doorway, nothing but a night of promised pleasure on the other side.

"Last chance," I whisper.

Not a second later, his lips are on mine, tasting mine. I moan in response and that one sound has him pushing me up against the door, one hard thigh between my legs as he continues to devour my mouth. I've never been kissed like this. Not ever. I can't get enough.

With one final peck, he says, "Does that answer your question?"

I nod quickly, my lips feeling puffy and bruised. Dear god, tonight is going to be phenomenal.

Hunter takes the keycard out of my hand and flashes it against the automatic lock. As the door opens, we step through, Hunter moving farther inside to glance around my room, while I lean my back against the door, still recovering from his kiss.

When he turns back to me and gives me that same smile most people don't see, I know for sure this night is going to happen. This isn't a movie star looking to score. This is Hunter, a man who is attracted to a woman and wants to spend the night getting to know her in every way.

Finding my courage, I push off of the door and whip my dress over my head tossing it aside as I step toward him. Standing before him in only a lacy thong and a simple strapless bra, which barely contains the girls, I wait for him to do something. To say something. Instead, Hunter's eyes widen as he takes me in. His eyes slowly move across my body. I'm not an overly confident woman but tonight, standing here before this man, I've never felt more beautiful. Reaching behind my back, I flick the clasp of my bra, letting it tumble to the floor.

I have one night with my dream man; I'm not wasting a second of it.

To hell with wedding clichés.

Chapter 11

Hunter

Is it still called a walk of shame when you feel anything but shame?

Leaving Celeste this morning was not easy. Her warm body curled around mine was pure heaven. Her skin warm against mine, the blonde spirals messy from our night of exploring one another. Thank goodness the hotel is discreet and able to provide condoms with a single phone call. The hours I spent familiarizing myself with every inch of her body should have exhausted me, but it seems to have had the opposite effect.

As we lie in bed, watching the sunrise, I suggested locking ourselves away for the morning, ordering room service and staying in that vacation bubble she mentioned last night. Then her alarm shattered that peaceful thought, reminding her she is supposed to meet up with Carrie before the new Mrs. Roberts leaves for her honeymoon. Since most guests arrived for the nuptials four days before I landed, they'll be leaving today as well. Everyone we know will be gone except Celeste and me. Since I couldn't make the trip days prior to the wedding, I settled for staying a few days longer. Celeste on the other hand, says she gets the best deals on less traveled days.

The green light unlocking my door flashes and I step into the room. Maybe if Celeste and I have a repeat of last night, I can convince her to come to my suite. Not that there was anything wrong with her room, but it seems ridiculous for me to have this huge space and not use it. Besides, there are more surfaces here for us to christen.

Walking into the bedroom, I toss my wallet on the dresser and kick off my shoes. As I unbutton my shirt, I see the red light on the hotel phone flashing. A message. I should ignore it. My phone is powered down for a reason. I need to relax. A thought of my parents unable to reach me is the only reason I pick up the receiver and listen to the message.

"Hunter why is your phone going to voicemail? Is it broken? Did something happen? I knew this was a bad idea."

Eddie rambles on. Asking questions and drawing his own conclusions. He is an excellent manager and I owe him my career, but the guy can't take a hint for shit. Hell, not even a hint. I flat out told him not to call me. I need forty-eight hours off. I guess he's doing that new math my nephew bitches about because I haven't been here forty-eight hours.

After the fifth message he seems to relent and accept I'm off the grid. "Fine. Look, there may be some scheduling changes in the next few weeks so make sure you check in with me when you're back stateside. Don't get too comfortable. Remember the press lurks in the shadows and someone you think is your friend may be using you. Don't hook up with any randoms either. We don't need your junk on the cover of the tabloids. Not that I mind extra press, but it's not the image we're going for."

With that final warning, I hang up the receiver and pad my way into the shower. Another bonus to this suite is the massive walk-in shower and multiple jets to work out the tight muscles in my back. Letting the hot water beat my skin, I drop my chin to my chest and replay last night in my mind.

Holding Celeste close to me as we swayed to the music, so far off the fast beat it was laughable, I was happy to stand in the middle of the space with eyes on us. Mostly Carrie's eyes as she waggled her brows and made kissy faces at Celeste. It was the first time in a long time I can truly say I didn't mind being front and center in a public space. Contrary to what some may think about actors, not all of us love being the center of attention unless it's on the stage or screen. Hand me a script and give me direction and I'll stand beneath the hot lights and act my ass off. I'll demand attention and relish in the accolades. The applause and words of affirmation filling my soul.

Yet, last night, still incognito to almost everyone thanks to my apparently lumberjack costume, I pretended not to notice the whispers, because I didn't care. I saw them, but for once, I didn't mind. Not when I know it was because they were looking at her. The way her body molded to mine and the way her blonde curls blew in the breeze.

Shaking off the memories of that hair feathered across her pillow as she looked up at me, I turn to the taps and crank the handles to cold, letting the switch in temperature calm my need to rush to her again.

These towels are plush and soft. No surprise there. This hotel doesn't skimp on anything, and with the price I'm paying for this room, I should hope not. Running the white cotton across my long hair, I use my other hand to wipe the mirror, now foggy from the steam. As I fasten the towel around my waist, I contemplate shaving off the beard. I can't do much about the too long hair on my head, but the beard is something I can handle. Except, I think Celeste may revoke her offer of a day on the beach today if I do. She made multiple mentions last night of the way it tickled her skin in the best way and I wouldn't want to deny her that. Nor would I want to deny myself seeing her in a bikini. The beard stays.

A knock at the door pulls my attention from my morning routine. Nobody knows my room number and I didn't call for room service but perhaps it's housekeeping. To my surprise it isn't a woman pushing a cart of linens. It's so much better.

"Hey gorgeous."

Bright pink tints her creamy skin and my heart thuds in my chest.

"Hi."

I purse my lips to hold back laughter at the way her eyes settle on the towel low on my hips. Her tongue peeks out between her lips, and if I'm not mistaken, her breath hiccups before she releases it and darts her eyes to mine.

Smirking her way, I step aside and motion her into the room.

"No way, mister. I step through that door and I'm going to do very wicked things. I just wanted to let you know I checked at the front desk and they do have open cabanas today."

"You could have called," I comment as I rest my hands on my hips, letting the door rest against my elbow.

"I don't have your cell number and if I had, I wouldn't have seen all of this." Her hand swirls between us like she's a magician and I'm her surprise for the audience.

Stepping into her space, I slide my hand around the back of her neck, my hands missing her curls since she has them piled atop her head. Leaning down, I smack a quick kiss to her lips.

"I'll book the cabana and meet you in the lobby in

thirty?"

Sighing, a small smile appears on her lips. "'Kay."

Once I'm left alone, I do as I said and book our cabana, having the staff add a few salads and snacks along with waters and other non-alcoholic beverages. Celeste and I may not have been drunk last night, but I know we both drank more than we normally do and could use a little hydration today.

The resort is bustling by the time I make it to the lobby to meet Celeste. She's standing near a large fountain talking to the Roberts family as I approach. Matthew spots me first, a knowing smile appearing on his lips. He can't see my eyes with my polarized sunglasses which is probably a good thing because if I could shoot lasers at him, I would.

"There he is. How're you feeling, whiskey man?"

Gripping his palm, I squeeze a little harder than necessary. "Is that my new superhero name? I don't think the studio would approve."

Carrie giggles as her new step-daughter tugs on my arm. Looking down at her, I wait for her to speak.

"Carrie and Miss Celeste said you're way hotter than on television. I don't know what the TV has to do with it, but our room had air conditioning that made it so cold I needed a blanket. Maybe you should use our room."

The adults around us bark out laughs, causing the pint size cutie to look at them like they've lost their minds before turning her attention back to me. I school my own laugh and say, "Thanks for the offer. I'll see what I can do."

Satisfied with my response, she skips away, and I look to Carrie and Celeste. Neither will look me in the eye as they suddenly find the water in the fountain much more exciting.

"Well, that was awkward. Ready, babe? We should claim our seats on the shuttle," Matthew suggests as he snuggles into his wife's neck, causing her to giggle. "You two play nice today. Hunter, I'll be in L.A. next month for a seminar if you want to meet up. It's for my day job so I'll be more than happy to get away from the suits for a while."

"Sounds good. Send me the dates and I'll see if I'm in town."

The happy couple strolls away, hand in hand leaving Celeste and me alone. This time, it's me who takes the time to peruse Celeste's body. The dress she is wearing should conceal her curves, but it doesn't. Instead, the deep V at her chest gives me a peek at her cleavage while the thin fabric, skims her hips before stopping just above her knee.

"Ready for a day of fun in the sun?" I ask as I grab her hand, interlinking our fingers.

The smile she gives me in response is worth more than the contract I just signed for a new ad campaign. Together, we make our way out to the beach and a day with no commitments and nowhere else to be but with each other.

"A rubber band pulled tight and set on fire. That's how my skin feels. I thought a cabana meant we would be shaded."

She flinches as I rub the aloe into her skin. Her very pink and hot skin. Hours playing like a couple of teenagers on spring break, we didn't do the one thing my mom always reminded me to do hourly—reapply sunscreen. What can I say? I was distracted by a hot blonde in a floral print bathing suit. While my dreams had Celeste in a tiny bikini, the real life version of her in a one-piece suit that hugged every curve and accentuated her lean legs was even better.

"It was all the time in the water that did us in."

"Not us. Me. You and your perfect "I can tan and never burn" skin tone are barely pink. My white ass is burnt like a piece of bacon."

Sitting before me with only a towel wrapped around her, I gently apply the aloe but watch as her warm skin absorbs it instantly. When we returned from the beach, I convinced Celeste to grab her belongings and move to my room. We're both flying out tomorrow morning, coincidentally enough, on the same flight, so there's no reason we can't spend our final night together and share my car to the airport. I immediately directed her to the large shower and set the water to cool, hoping to pull some of the heat from her skin.

"Okay that's enough for now," I say, snapping the

aloe vera bottle shut. "I think it's just the initial burn, nothing major. It wouldn't surprise me if the sting was gone by morning. Thankfully, we don't have to leave this room. We can order dinner, cue up a movie, and never leave this bed."

Turning around and searching my eyes, she lifts her lips into a smile. "I love when you talk dirty. Will it bother you if I slip between these cool sheets and take off this towel? It's driving me nuts, but I don't think I can put on a shirt let alone a bra."

"Would you being naked in my bed bother me? Have we met?"

Rolling her eyes, she slowly moves to the bed and slips between the sheets, tossing her towel on the floor. I scoop it up, hand her the remote, and leave her alone while I go shower the day off myself.

A dinner of burgers and fries with two flavors of milkshakes behind us, we're halfway through a classic romantic comedy of Celeste's choosing when I notice she's quieter than usual. Looking down to where she's settled at my side, I find her sound asleep. Gently, I slide out from next to her and she turns to her side, hugging the pillow to her chest.

Quietly, I clean up our mess and use the bathroom before killing the lights and sliding in next to her, spooning her to my front. The heat from her sunburn is warm on my chest and a reminder of a weekend that has reset my soul. I have the woman in my arms to thank for that.

Chapter 12

Celeste

The warmth of the tropical breeze blows over my naked skin. It's soothing and relaxes me in a way nothing in the city has for months. As I stretch out the kinks of a night of amazing sex and a good night's sleep, I enjoy the bright sunlight shining in the room. That can only mean one thing… this day is going to be great.

No, that's not right. It means something else. But what?

"OHMIGOD WE OVERSLEPT!"

Between my outburst and my Olympic track-and-field-like launch out of bed, Hunter wakes up.

He sits straight up in bed, eyes wide and assessing. "What? What's wrong?"

"It's eight forty-five! We have to leave for the airport, like, now!"

"Son of bitch," he grumbles and slowly rolls off the world's most comfortable mattress as if we aren't about to miss our flight to Atlanta. I assume we'll part ways for our connecting flights, but I don't have time to think about that right now.

"What? Why aren't you moving faster?" I ask as I pull on my bra, hissing at the sting of my sunburn as the clasp snaps in place. So much for my skin being healed by morning.

Picking up the phone, he presses the one for the concierge. Is he ordering room service? We don't have time for this. "Yeah, we are running late for check out. Myself and Celeste Pump… Pumpa…"

"Pumperkin!" I yell.

"Right. What she said. I have a driver waiting for me downstairs. Can you please tell him we'll be about ten minutes?"

Hunter gives them more information so we can check out quickly and then hangs up, turning to me. "There. Fixed."

"That was so much easier than trying to catch the shuttle to the airport," I admit, throwing clothes into my suitcase willy nilly.

"Stick with me, baby, and we'll go places." He waggles his eyebrows, apparently not realizing he just quoted The Lion King, not Casablanca. I'd find it cheesy. Instead it's just another endearing part of this man I have enjoyed so much.

"While you have mad skills on getting our transportation cleared up, Hunter, it's still a thirty minute drive to the airport and we have to check in, get through International security and find our gate. All in less than two and a half hours. Got a magic wand for that?"

The way he crinkles his nose makes me pause. He does, doesn't he? The man is about to pull out some more magic, I just know it.

"We're already checked in and have priority boarding. Plus the driver will have TSA waiting to escort us through the airport so we make it on time."

I drop the shirt I just picked up off the floor. "What do you mean they'll escort us?"

He shrugs sheepishly, and I don't think the beginnings of a sunburn is pinking his cheeks. Nope. That's a blush. "It's sort of a celebrity perk. That way we can get in and out of the airport fast without having to stop and look at directions or signs. Keeps us from getting stopped by fans."

"Well, well," I say playfully. "Isn't that a nice addition to this vacation. In that case, I'll take the extra two minutes to actually fold my clothes instead of shoving them inside my suitcase."

He smiles and gestures over his shoulder with his thumb. "I'll use the facilities first and grab all my toiletries, then we can switch. We'll make it, I promise."

My head cocks to the side as I watch him saunter away from me. That man has one fine back and shoulders. The muscles he sports are possibly my favorite part of his body. Well, second favorite part.

As soon as he's out of sight and I can keep myself focused, I move at a steady pace, and it's a good thing we don't dawdle. By the time we're dressed, clear out of the room, and find our driver, we have less than two hours until take off. We are not going to be at the airport three hours ahead of schedule like the airlines recommend. Knowing how close we're cutting it stresses me out. At least I can pull up my boarding pass on my phone and make sure my ID is handy.

But of course, there's another problem.

"Shit."

"What?" Hunter leans over to see what has me freaking out this time.

"Something's wrong with my reservation. The ticket I pulled up has me in first class." I laugh as I search around the app to see how to fix it. "That is way out of my paygrade. I should be in the back over the engine. Probably in a middle seat next to a screaming baby."

Hunter doesn't laugh with me. Instead he tenses up. There's that faux sunburn on his cheeks again.

"So, um…" He clears his throat like he's nervous. "I took the liberty of upgrading you to first class so we could sit together. But only if you want to," he tacks on quickly.

I am a strong, independent woman. I can take care of myself and pride myself on the fact that I've been able to survive and thrive in one of the most expensive cities in the world. But knowing that Hunter has enjoyed getting to know me, that he's enjoyed spending time with me so much that he dropped at least two grand so I can sit next to him in luxury for a few hours has my heart melting. I knew I felt this thing between us but wasn't holding out hope for much more. If it ends up being a weekend fling, I'm okay with that. But to know he finds our budding relationship, whatever status it is, easy and something he wants more of makes me smile.

"I'd like that. Thank you."

The relief on his face is evidence of his nerves in even offering. And once again, I find myself endeared by Hunter the man. If only our real lives weren't so far apart in not only distance but life situation. Bummer.

Pulling up to the airport, I grab my purse just as the driver opens our door. As promised, a very large man who is muscular in all the right places, and based off his uniform works for security, is standing at the curb.

"Mr. Stone." He holds his hand out to shake. "My name is Raf and I'll be helping you and your party to the gate today. Do you have any bags that need checking?"

Before Hunter or I can reply, the driver drops our luggage next to us. Raf signals another airport employee to grab our items. Speaking quickly and in hushed tones, he directs them to which flight is ours and they're off with our suitcases, only pausing to hand us the tags to claim them later.

"Thank you, Raf. Is that short for something?" I ask as I slip the tag into my purse.

"Rafael, miss. Only my mother and wife use my full name. Usually if I'm in some sort of trouble."

Smiling at the kind man, I glance to my travel partner and notice he's donned a baseball cap which is pulled low on his forehead. I watch as everyone scurries around us, seemingly unaware of the celebrity in their midst. Holy shit. Hunter wasn't kidding when he eluded to it being red carpet service. Here I was worried about missing our flight and they're going above and beyond to make sure we don't just get there on time, we do it without any stress. It's like nothing I've ever experienced.

Hunter Stone, on the other hand, fits in seamlessly as he discreetly passes a folded bill to our driver and his sincere thanks for getting us here on time. I don't want to know how much the gratuity was. The way all of this is happening, I wouldn't be surprised if it was an amount close to my last light bill. I've learned in the last few days with him that Hunter isn't just a movie star, he's so much more. But when it's time to put his fame to use, he does it well.

By the time we cut to the front of the long security line, courtesy of our new pal Raf, and arrive at the gate, our plane is already boarding. As priority members, Hunter not me, we bypass the passengers waiting in the general boarding line and quickly make our way to the ticket handler. It's fast but with our VIP treatment, we are settled into our plush seats within minutes.

"That was incredible. I've never had airport service like that before," I say as I fasten my seatbelt and explore all the amenities in the lavish area they call first class. Not only does the tray table fold out from the arm, there's a phone charger right next to me. *And* the seat lies almost all the way back! I need to save up more points on my credit card because this is definitely the way to travel from now on.

"It definitely makes traveling a lot nicer, that's for sure."

"I bet if we were running any later they would even hold the plane for you."

Shaking his head, he adjusts the cap on his head and twists in his seat, facing me. The plane begins to fill with passengers, the volume increasing tremendously. I lean forward, the movement shifting my shirt and sending a stabbing pain through my shoulder.

"What's wrong?" Hunter asks me, concern written all over his beautiful face. Or I assume so. I can't really see much of his face with that damn hat.

"Sunburn. I kind of forgot about it for a minute. Have no fear, it has reminded me."

Reaching over, he grabs my hand, holding it in his much larger one and leans his head back, eyes closed. "Next time, I'll remind you to wear sunscreen."

He said next time. Like we're going to frolic in the ocean again. Together. Obviously, I'm delirious. Who uses the word "frolic" anyway?

"Hunter Stone, you have spoiled me." I may or may not be wiggling in my seat. I don't think I can ever go back to sitting in basic economy. Who could after experiencing such plush seats?

Laughing, he adjusts the overhead air blower not bothering to respond. I think it's actually called an air vent, but it blows air so hard and loud I like calling it a blower. Our layover was long enough for us to grab a drink and eat a leisurely lunch in the private airline lounge. This time, I didn't have to beg for entrance. Nope, being on Hunter's arm and with a first class ticket meant I was greeted with open arms.

Okay, not actual open arms. They weren't handing out hugs. This has been one heck of a bonus to an already awesome long weekend in the tropics. A girl could get used to this life.

"I can't believe we're both headed to New York," I comment as I fasten my seatbelt. Hunter, on the other hand is taking his sweet time getting settled. "What do you have there? An interview with Kelly and whoever her current co-host is or something?"

He looks up to the ceiling and puffs out a breath. "Shit. I'm so sorry, Celeste. I keep forgetting about that interview I promised you."

I wave him off. "It's not a big deal."

"It's a very big deal. I don't want anyone to scoop you."

I flash him an incredulous look. "I'd hardly say one of the most popular talk shows on television interviewing the biggest and, if I'm honest, hottest actor is "scooping" my little blog. It's what they do. I'm just an opportunist," I joke. "But seriously. I'm truly not worried about it right now. We're still in vacation mode so just relax. Do you want to watch a movie?" I ask him as I scroll through the screen to find something we'd both enjoy watching.

Hunter doesn't respond, just digs around in his carry-on, looking for something.

"What's wrong?"

"Hmm? Oh nothing. I just feel a headache coming on. Here it is." He pulls out a Tylenol bottle and shakes it at me in victory. "The cabin pressure will make it worse if I don't take something now." He opens his prize and shakes some pills out into his hand. Only that's not Tylenol.

"Um… what exactly are you taking?"

"Tylenol. I have a headache."

"But there are four different kinds of pills there."

He looks down and smiles. "Oh that. Yeah, it's a bad habit I picked up from my mother. Instead of taking a bunch of different bottles she just keeps them all in the same one. Don't worry, I know what they are."

"None of them are illegal are they?"

He purses his lips at me like I'm the one engaging in strange behavior right now. I don't think he's dependent on any drugs, or at least I didn't see him partake in anything this weekend. Well, he likely drank all the whiskey at the bar at the wedding reception but other than that, he didn't seem to have any vices. I'm going to be really pissed if I missed him slipping pills. I may have engaged in a one-weekend-stand with an almost stranger, but I still consider myself an excellent judge of character. I better not be off my game.

"I can see why you might think that, but I promise it's only over the counter meds. Don't worry. My headache is already going away."

In four seconds? Unlikely. But I have no reason to doubt him, so I let it go and focus on the joy of flying first class. It really lives up to its name. Almost immediately upon taking off, a flight attendant comes by and offers us free alcoholic beverages. Not wanting to disappoint her, I take her up on the offer and enjoy a lovely mimosa. Why it tastes better coming from a tiny bottle into a champagne flute on an airplane, I'll never know. It's almost too bad Hunter fell asleep before the wheels left the ground. He's missing out.

Enjoying my drink and a paranormal book Carrie recommended about a haunted house and the ghost that lives inside it, pining for the one she loves, I'm startled when Hunter moans next to me.

Dropping my device, I turn toward him. "Hunter?"

He moans again. This time he opens his eyes but there's something very strange about his expression. He looks almost blank. Like the lights are on but no one is home. Probably the lights in the ghost house I'm reading about.

Holy shit, did my book just come to life?

"Carrie put you up to this, didn't she? She's trying to scare the bejeezus out of me by making me read this scary book and then having you act the part of the walking dead. I knew I shouldn't have told her about my neighbor coming home drunk while I was reading a book about zombies. I just handed her the idea. I'm right, aren't I?"

He looks around, but I'm not sure what he's seeing. He's not all there, and I'm almost positive he's not understanding a word I'm saying.

"You better not be playing, Hunter. This isn't funny."

The flight attendant who has been keeping a close eye on her passengers and making sure we're all happy approaches. "Is everything okay, Miss?"

"Um… I'm not sure. He's acting really strange. He said he was taking a Tylenol but he must have taken the wrong thing."

"Do you know what he took?"

"I don't know. He said none of it was illegal, so maybe a pain killer or something?"

On cue, Hunter stands up, takes one look at me and climbs onto my lap.

What the hell is happening here. Is he… ohmigod is he purring like a cat? It's a damn good thing this man is incognito. I have a feeling Eddie wouldn't be too pleased about Hunter ruining his image by pretending he's a feline. A lion might be okay, but this is definitely not that. He's way too docile.

Our flight attendant seems suddenly less concerned about Hunter and more irritated. "Oh boy. I hate it when people take Ambien on airplanes."

"You think that's what it was?"

"He's licking his own hands. I guarantee that's what it was."

Well shit. She's right. Now he's grooming himself. If he sticks his leg up in the air and goes for his balls, he's on his own.

"So what do I do?"

"Just let him be," she advises. "As long as he's not irritating the other passengers, taking off his clothes, or trying to break into the cockpit, he'll be fine."

"Great," I say through gritted teeth. I'm thrilled Hunter upgraded me to this giant chair and all, but at this point I'd have more room if I was sitting in that middle seat in the back I had reserved.

The flight feels like twice as long as it did going the other direction, probably because of the oversized kitty sitting on top of me. But eventually he curls up enough that I can grab my device and distract myself with my ghost again. Man, what I wouldn't give to have this plane be haunted instead of being a human-sized cat rescue.

Fortunately for me, when it's finally time to descend, the flight attendant and I are able to coax him back into his seat and get his seatbelt on. He's awake now, but still so out of it. It's almost as if he's drunk, just staring out the window. Until suddenly he sees me.

"Hey, Celeste! I had no idea you would be on this plane! How cool is that?"

"Super cool, Hunter."

"Where are you going?"

"I'm going home."

Wait. Hold on. I'm going home. But *where the hell is Hunter going?*

"Hunter," I say gently, hoping to hold his attention. "Where are you going?"

"Wherever you are, baby." And then he starts belting out an old Bryan Adams song, much to the delight of our favorite flight attendant, who is probably thrilled that we're almost to the gate and not going to be her responsibility anymore. Which means he's my responsibility now. Craaaaaaap.

"Hunter." He keeps singing. "Hunter!" I try again but no response. "Hunter!" I slap his arm this time. He looks at me in surprise.

"Hey, Celeste! I had no idea you would be on this plane! How cool is that?"

Oh god. Now he's having short term memory loss. Amazing.

"Let me see your phone, Hunter."

He hands it over with a smile and goes back to

singing about ringing his bell. I'm not even trying to make heads or tails of this anymore. I just need to see if maybe his email has his flight itinerary. Worst case, I can find Eddie's phone number and he can help me out.

Pressing the power button, I wait a few seconds until it starts dinging like mad. The phone makes more noise than Hunter with the way it's blowing up. I don't think I've ever seen anyone have this many notifications before.

Hunter gives the phone a dirty look, like it's offended him. "That's why I turned it off. I hate that sound."

Trying to swipe it open, I'm out of luck. "Do you know the password?"

He opens his mouth to answer me, pausing to tap his chin and quirk his lips from one side to the other. I wait… and wait until his brain catches up. "Nope."

I drop my head back onto my seat. "Hunter, how can I get you where you're supposed to be if I don't know where you're going and when?"

"I'm going somewhere?" And then he catches my eyes again. "Hey, Celeste! I had no idea you would be on this plane!"

"I know, I know, super cool, whatever." I wave him off as I try a couple random combinations. Not that I could be so lucky, but it was worth a shot.

Shaking my head, I realize there is only one option. "Welp, looks like you're going home with me, tonight, Hunter Stone."

His face lights up for half a second before he attempts a sultry look. He fails miserably. "We're going back to your place, huh?"

"Don't get your hopes up, lover boy. You need to sleep it off." Holding my hand out I add, "Now hand me your wallet."

"Okay," he says with no hesitation and slaps it right in my palm. Good thing I thought of that before a thief did. "What do you need my wallet for?"

"You're rich. You're paying for a cab and tomorrow you're going to thank me for not taking pictures and selling them to the paps. Now let's go."

As the doors finally open, I gather all our belongings, his included and race to catch up with Hunter, who is now skipping down the jetway into the terminal.

This is going to be a long night. Good thing he's cute.

Chapter 13

Hunter

Letting out a low grumble, I untangle myself from the sheet that is wrapped around my leg like a tourniquet. What the hell did I eat before bed last night? Nothing comes to mind but whatever it was, I know it gave me some seriously weird dreams. When my leg is finally free of its captor, I look around, taking stock of my surroundings. Things are a little fuzzy, like I'm drunk which I guess I could be. My lack of memory indicates one hell of a bender.

This bed isn't nearly as comfortable as the one at the resort but the woman next to me is a pleasant surprise. Last thing I remember was getting on an airplane in Atlanta. We should have parted ways in New York so it's nice to see I have a little more time with her. Even if I can't remember why.

I scan the room for some clue as to where we are. It's a small space, the bed pushed up against a wall, a single window near our feet. Darkness blankets the space with only a sliver of light streaming in through a space between the curtains.

My eyes focus more, and I can make out Celeste next to me. Her blonde hair is loose and free, like her spirit. She's quiet. Too quiet in fact. Because one can never be too sure, I stick my hand up to her face to make sure she is breathing. Exhaling in relief that she's alive, I slowly reach my hand out to rest it on her hip before laying my head back down on the pillow.

My time in paradise was supposed to offer me rest and relaxation. I think I slept less the last few days than I did the weeks prior. Only, I'm not tired from the late nights. My body is still exhausted but my mind is rested. That's the result of losing hours of sleep to be with Celeste. I have no regrets about that.

Yawning, I don't fight the sleep as it pulls me under. I need to sleep off whatever I drank. I can only hope the second half of my night isn't spent dreaming of tuna and sandy beaches. Not that I minded the beaches at the resort but the version in my dreams was a lot more abrasive on my dream feet.

I don't know how long I slept but the way my bladder feels, it was long enough for me to be at maximum capacity. Untangling myself from the bedsheet, I glance a look at Celeste. She's turned to her side with her back to me. I stop myself from reaching out to touch her. The sunburn on her shoulders looks lighter than yesterday. I have no recollection of making it here last night and the time I did wake up is nothing but a mishmash of memories, but from the looks of things we are at her apartment.

Standing to my full height, I rotate my neck, working out a kink, and note I'm only in a pair of boxer briefs. I also take a quick glance around the room and am surprised to see it isn't really a room but more of a space closed off by a curtain. It has the makings of a bedroom but with only three walls instead of four. In the corner is a small desk with stacks of papers and a plant that looks like it needs more than water to bring it back to life. Her dresser is organized to perfection while still piled high with knickknacks and pictures. It's comforting and everything I'd expect from Celeste. Slipping past the curtain, I spy the open door at the end of the short hallway and beeline for the bathroom.

I hate to say it, but this bathroom is the size of my shower in L.A. My condo isn't huge by any means, but it is a decent two bedroom and two bathrooms with a balcony. My master bathroom is nice and modern. The opposite of this one. I think if I reached out both arms I could easily touch each wall with my fingertips.

The nostalgia hits me in the gut. This is exactly like the place I lived in during my early acting years. When I was going on audition after audition and praying for my big break. When I starred in that play that was so far off Broadway, you would need GPS to find it. The same one that Celeste has the playbill for.

Washing my hands and splashing cold water on my face, I open the medicine cabinet hoping to find toothpaste or mouthwash. I'm in luck when I find a tube of toothpaste. Using my finger, I brush the disgusting taste from my mouth. Seriously, what did I eat? More importantly, what did I drink?

While I try to figure out what items I need to add to the "never again" list, I pad my way through the small apartment, taking in the little couch and table in the living room. A nice size television sits on top of what looks like an old dresser. That's it. Not much else to see. Just past the living room is a small kitchen. I glance at the clock. It's just after six in the morning. This is far earlier than I would normally be awake but here I am.

What are the chances Celeste and her roommate have coffee and maybe some food to throw together a little breakfast? Opening the refrigerator, I take in the options. A pizza box, salsa, a lime, and a jar of pickles. Okay so no breakfast. I spy a French press on the counter near the sink and a can of coffee next to it. Now we're talking. In the dish drainer is a pan and two coffee cups. Filling the pan with water, I place it on the stove to boil and go about preparing the coffee.

Thankfully, the French press is manual just like the one we used to use for camping, and I won't disturb Celeste while she sleeps with unnecessary noise. When the water shows signs it's hot but not quite boiling, I turn off the burner and fill the press and let it sit for a few minutes while I try to find something to eat. Pickles for breakfast aren't the worst thing in the world but certainly not my first choice.

I feel like a creep opening cupboards, but I know there has to be something here. Cereal or oatmeal. Maybe even a can of soup. I'm not choosy at this point. Just hungry. With one failed cupboard after another, I finally strike gold, okay maybe more like bronze, but regardless I found food. Or kind of. It's a Twinkie. Since those things will last one hundred years or something crazy, I'm going for it.

Ripping off the wrapper, I take a bite and begin chewing as I also lower the press's plunger, watching as the clear water becomes coffee. With one hand slowly plunging, I lift the gooey pastry to my mouth and then almost die by choking when I hear a scream.

"Who are you?"

Abandoning my coffee, I turn to face the woman who stands in the doorway, a can of pepper spray aimed at me and a crazed look on her face.

"I'm Hunter," I reply through the mouthful of deliciousness.

Her eyes flick from me to the light yellow treat in my hand. I am an actor. I work with other actors. It isn't uncommon to witness them turn from one persona to another. Yet, I don't think I've seen anyone go from crazed to enraged so quickly.

"Is that my Twinkie?" she shrieks.

I open my mouth to respond when the curtain that

makes up Celeste's door opens.

"Anna?"

Never taking her eyes off me, the woman I now know is Anna asks, "Why is there a lumberjack in our apartment?"

Looking past her shoulder at Celeste I drop my shoulders in shame. "I really need to shave, don't I?"

Celeste shrugs. "I told you it was a little Paul Bunyan chic. You opted not to listen."

"Wait," Anna says, dropping her pepper spray to her side. I relax at the gesture, feeling like I just dodged a bullet. "You're Hunter Stone."

Pushing past her, Celeste snorts a laugh before stepping up next to me and whispering, "Good morning. Do I smell coffee?"

Smiling down at her I nod just as Anna speaks, pulling both of our attention. "Hunter Stone is in our apartment. In his underwear. It must be five o'clock somewhere, get the whiskey and make my coffee Irish."

I knew I was in my boxers when I started my quest for coffee and breakfast but in the chaos of the almost pepper spraying, I forgot. I'm also having regrets for my consumption of the Twinkie. I don't remember this weird after taste from when I was a kid.

"So I'm just going to…"

"Your luggage is at the foot of my bed."

"Thank you," I say as I squat down to eye level with Celeste before placing a quick peck to her lips.

As I step away Anna whisper shouts, "Ohmy-fuhreakinggod Lumberjack Hunter Stone kissed you!"

Laughing to myself, I make my way into Celeste's room and rummage through my things for a pair of jeans. As I'm fastening the button, I see my phone on the desk plugged in. I'm still not ready to face the real world and turn my back on it. Maybe if I do that, it'll go away. Or at the very least, I can pretend I didn't know where it is.

Slapping on some deodorant and tugging on a T-shirt, I make my way back out to the kitchen area and find both women with a cup of coffee in their hand. Leaning close, I can tell Celeste is catching Anna up on the weekend. I know this because Anna keeps smacking Celeste and saying "Holy shit" each time.

"How's the sunburn?" I ask, announcing my appearance. The ladies jump apart, guilt written across both their faces.

"A lot better. Here, I took a sip."

I accept the cup from Celeste and slide up next to her. Being together this weekend was seamless, but we were also alone most of the time. We haven't actually been together, affectionate, in front of other people but until she smacks me away, I'm going to enjoy every minute I get to touch her.

"I'm going to excuse myself and change while you two… well whatever."

Anna leaves us alone and scurries down the hall to the actual room with a door. When the door clicks closed I turn to Celeste.

"So, how exactly did I end up here and do you know why I'm craving a tuna sandwich?"

Chapter 14

Celeste

"You don't remember anything about our flight from Atlanta, do you?"

I can tell he's trying hard to remember something, anything, but he's coming up blank. Good thing I have enough memory for both of us. And oh, what fun memories they are.

"I… I don't." He shakes his head, likely trying to sort out whatever fuzzy thoughts he can't totally grasp. "How much did I drink?"

I take a sip of coffee before answering. I'm not angry at him. Not even close. But as a lover of stories, I want to make sure my comedic timing is just right. It's not every day you get to tell a celebrity they may want to avoid getting a pet cat, and not because he travels too much to take proper care of it, but because they may be too close to kindred spirits.

"You didn't drink anything."

"I didn't?"

I shake my head.

"Did I get drugged or something?" The sudden realization has his eyes widening in horror. "Ohmigod, did someone drug me so they could take pictures? Holy shit. Does Eddie know? Is he on it already? Tell me I kept my clothes on."

Well damn. My comedic timing didn't take in account that he might skip right over the truth and go straight into panic mode.

He rushes to my room and since our apartment is the size of a postage stamp, returns before I can swallow my coffee. Hunter's panic is evident as he taps at the screen of his phone. Come to think of it, this is the first time I've seen him looking for it all weekend. I know he's been avoiding it so before he blows his self-imposed technology hiatus, I stop him.

"No one drugged you, Hunter. And I promise there are no pictures anywhere. Although I may have missed out on opportunity for some playful blackmail myself."

Hunter turns to me, his eyes darkening. "There is no such thing as playful blackmail."

It seems that's a hot button issue. "You're right. I'm sorry. What I mean is you can stop freaking out. No one drugged you." Well, except maybe himself. "There are no pictures. No one even knows you're here. I was very stealth, and your vacation outfit seems to have done the trick."

His whole body relaxes and as I suspected, he tosses aside that phone he's been avoiding. Rubbing his hands down his face he takes a deep, centering breath. "Then how did I get here and why don't I remember anything?"

Putting my mug down, I lean back against the counter, my flannel jammie shirt sliding down one shoulder. "You had a headache."

"Right. So I took some Tylenol."

I shake my head. "That wasn't Tylenol, Hunter."

And just like that, a proverbial lightbulb goes off over his head. "I got it mixed up with Ambien, didn't I?"

"That is our suspicion."

He groans and plops down on one of two bar stools next to our tiny island. "I can't believe I accidentally drugged myself."

Laughing lightly, I walk to him and rub my hand down his back. "That you did, my friend. You're just lucky I was sitting with you to help keep you contained."

"Wait." His head pops up and I have to step back quickly to avoid being nailed in the face. "You said 'our' suspicion. Who is 'our'?"

"Let's just say the flight attendant was less than happy to have a human-sized cat batting around some airline issued headphones with his man-sized paw at thirty thousand feet."

His eyes close slowly and blush covers the entirety of his face. "That explains my craving for a tuna fish sandwich."

I can't help it. My laugh comes out loud and lasts way too long. But now that I'm not worried he'll accidentally ram open an emergency exit as he chases a bit of fluff across the aisle of the plane, the entire thing is really funny. For me, anyway. Hunter doesn't quite see the humor in it yet.

Wiping the tears from my eyes, I fill in a few more blanks. "You spent most of the time curled up on my lap, grooming your paws."

His nose wrinkles like it's the most disgusting thing he's ever heard, and he jumps up, crossing the tiny area to the sink to wash his hands. "That is so gross. But you're sure there's not pictures?"

"Positive," I say, hoping the strength in my voice reassures him of just how confident I am this will stay between us and the poor traumatized flight attendant.

Wiping his hands on a tea towel, he tosses it on the counter and leans toward me. "Thank you, Celeste. I'm so sorry I grabbed the wrong pill."

"This is why most mothers abandon the whole putting all the pills in one bottle thing."

He huffs a small laugh. "I think I may need to do that as well. That would have been disastrous if I were by myself. And since you have no food in this place, can I take you out to breakfast? You said you live in Brooklyn, right?"

I nod.

"I know a really great luncheonette style place and I could go for an egg and cheese sandwich."

At the mention of food, my stomach growls. "Let me take a quick shower first. I didn't want to leave you alone last night to rinse the plane off me. I was afraid you'd head out one of the windows to go dumpster diving."

Finally, seeing the humor, he holds back a smirk. "You have no idea how much I appreciate that. I'd offer to shower with you, but I've been in your bathroom and I don't think we'd both fit in there."

I unattractively snort a laugh. "Yeah, Anna tried that one time."

"Tried what?" My roommate's long, unruly dark hair swings violently as she whips her head around her door frame.

Feigning offense, I gasp and grab at my chest. "Excuse you, were you spying on me?"

"Nope. I was spying on him."

"That's kind of rude."

"I agree. But it's not every day we have a celebrity turned skivvies-clad-lumberjack in our apartment." She makes a valid point and then her eyes narrow. "Plus, he already ate my Twinkie. I'm making sure he doesn't find my hidden Ding Dong."

Of course Hunter gasps with delight. "You have a Ding Dong?" He turns to riffle through the cabinets again.

"Hands off, Stone," Anna yells and comes barreling out of her room. "She may not have pictures of your Ambien haze but how do you know I don't?"

Hunter immediately freezes.

"Now back away from the cabinet," she instructs. He immediately complies. "And go sit on Celeste's bed like a good kitty."

I shake my head at the two of them. I'm not sure what's happening here but whatever it is, this might be the weirdest conversation that's ever happened in this apartment. And I lived here when Anna went through her Emo phase and she talked to my plant regularly because she just knew it had feelings.

Come to think of it, that plant has been looking pretty pekid since she stopped singing Janis Joplin songs to it every night before bed. Maybe she was onto something.

Regardless, I need to shower off two days of sun and sweat so they can continue playing whatever weird cat and mouse game they want while I get ready.

Leaning back in my chair, I put my hands over my overinflated stomach. It's probably not that big, but that's at least how I feel.

"I am stuffed."

Hunter barely looks up at me, still chowing down. Not only did he convince me to get the egg and cheese sandwich, he ordered us a veggie boat to share and some amazing lemonade with a kick. As meals not in the tropics go, it was pretty damn perfect.

Anna's going to kick herself for missing out on this so she could work on some song she's trying to perfect. Although Hunter did promise to bring back an entire box of Twinkies to replace her one. That was good enough for her.

"Can I ask you a question?"

He nods and continues to eat. When he mentioned knowing about this place he didn't say he used to come here often. But with the way he feels at home amongst the small tables and pastel wallpaper, somehow I just know this is one of the places he left behind that he actually misses.

"You haven't called anyone to let them know you're in New York. Are you hiding from something?"

Hunter takes a long drink of his lemonade, wipes his mouth and sighs, leaning back in his own seat.

"I'm not hiding necessarily. I'm just not interested in going back yet."

"How come?"

"I'm exhausted. With the movie junket and re-shoots for the show, I'm tapped out. Five days away from all the…" He stops, looking off in the distance, searching for his words and I sense an internal struggle that he doesn't want to share right now. "I just need to rest for a bit longer."

I nod in understanding. I get it, to a degree. Life can be draining sometimes. Not that I've had that same problem as of late. My problem is more one of wondering when the busyness will begin.

"You're welcome to stay as long as you need." I lower my chin so I can peek at him through my lashes. "I'm not kicking you out of my bed until you're ready to go."

He pauses as he lifts his glass to his lips and blinks once. "How often is Anna home?"

"Right now? Too often. She travels a lot to gigs in the tri-state area. But of course she's off this week."

"Drat." Finally getting that drink, he places his glass back down on the table just as my phone rings.

I don't recognize the number, but if I've learned anything over the years of trying to make a name for myself in this city, you always answer the phone. Sure, it's most likely going to be a telemarketer, but on the off-chance it's a job, I don't want to miss it.

I glance up at Hunter who has understanding written all over his face. "Answer it," he encourages, and I admit a part of me is relieved he still remembers enough about this world to understand why I have to answer a call during a lunch date.

Swiping, I use my most professional and "no I haven't been drinking hard lemonade" voice. "Hello."

"Hey Celeste, it's Manuel."

"Oh, hey there."

Manuel Hernandez and I worked on a small show last year. He as director, me as stage manager. Our styles really meshed and we both said we'd love to work together again at some point. My heart kicks up a notch, hoping this call means it's sooner rather than later.

"Listen, I was hired to direct a show at Northston Theater and I'm needing a stage manager asap."

"Su….sure." I stumble over my words as my excitement builds. Hunter's big hand comes over mine, steadying me. "That's no problem. When do you need me there?"

"Well, that's the thing."

Oh no. Nothing ever good comes after a sentence like that.

"We need you now. Today. Like in two hours, tops."

My jaw drops open. "Two hours? That's not a lot of notice, Manuel."

"I know, I know. And I'm sorry about that. The producers had someone else in mind but after meeting with her… well, it wasn't the best fit. Our personalities are too different. I've been calling you for a few days, but each call went straight to voicemail. This was my last ditch effort."

International calling isn't exactly part of my phone plan. I don't exactly love knowing I'm the theater's second choice, but I ignore that part. A job is a job, no matter how you get it.

"So will you do it?"

"Of course I'll do it!"

He cheers on the other end of the line and my eyes shoot across the table to Hunter. The smile on his face is huge as he raises his arm in and thrusts it overhead. A fist pump I'm going to pretend didn't just happen. Returning his smile, I watch as he stands and heads toward the counter, presumably to track down the check and pay up. I'm excited to get to work but I don't want to abandon Hunter. I know my time with him is limited and I don't want to miss a second of it.

As soon as I have that thought, I realize there's an easy solution. Manuel is rambling on and while I should be listening, my eyes continue to track my date.

"I have one small request," I add on making Manuel groan.

"I really don't know if I can meet any demands, Celeste. This is a small theater, not Broadway," he reasons.

"No, no. Nothing like that," I assure. "Well, two requests actually. I have to run back home and grab my kit because you know I can't work without all my supplies. I'm not using those paper shredders you call pens on my notebooks. So I might be a couple minutes late."

"Fine, fine. I know how you get without your beloved ball points and multi-colored highlighters.

What's the second?"

I have a friend in town who actually works in the industry and we're having brunch. Can I bring him with me? Just for today. I don't want to leave him sitting in my apartment."

Manuel pauses and I can practically hear the wheels churning in his head in contemplation. Director's don't like when people visit their closed theaters. Especially so early in the process. But I'm not leaving Hunter behind, not when theater was his first love. Somehow I know he needs to be there.

"Fine," he relents with a huff. "But you get to keep an eye on him, and you still have to get your job done. I'm not here to babysit or answer questions about my process. We've got work to do."

"Understood."

We hash out a few more details and he gives me the address of the rehearsal space we'll be using for a while. Before I know it, I hang up and clutch my phone to my heart.

It's a small theater. *Very* small. But it's a job in the industry I'm passionate about. A chance for me to do what I love. To me, it's a huge win.

Hunter strolls back over and grabs his jacket off the back of the chair. "We're good to go. You have somewhere to be."

"About that," I say, leaning my arms on the table. "How would you like to go check out the newest play to hit Northston Theater with me?"

His smile widens and I know that's a resounding yes.

145

Chapter 15

Hunter

I miss New York. The hustle and bustle of the city. The electricity that buzzes around you as you dodge others on the city sidewalks. Hell, I even find the blaring sirens and horns honking nostalgic. Los Angeles is a nice city but it's one that you don't spend time in. No, it's more like the city passes you by as you drive. And drive.

Here, taking public transportation and walking forces you to see what is around you. Beyond the architecture and personalities, it's the small things that remind you that you're in the greatest city in the world. As we walk side by side toward the subway, I reach over and grab Celeste's hand, interlacing our fingers. She stumbles and then grumbles a series of swear words. I never falter, just smile, knowing I keep her on her toes. Or, more like stumbling over her toes. Whatever.

With my ballcap pulled low on my forehead, I have managed to stay pretty invisible to most people. The dark sunglasses and beard don't hurt the effort. Although, I doubt anyone would expect to see me in New York. I'm known as a Hollywood guy these days. Just the thought of that makes me exhale loudly. The sound catches Celeste's attention, her gaze darting to mine. Instead of words to respond, I simply squeeze her hand as we rush down the steps.

Once we've swiped our metro cards granting us access to the platform, I release Celeste's hand and wrap my arm around her shoulders, holding her close. She rests her arm around my waist and peers up at me. Her big blue eyes remind me of the water in Turks and Caicos. Endless and full of possibility.

"You're quite affectionate today, Mr. Stone."

"Does it bother you?" I ask, worry lacing my question.

"Not at all. It surprises me a little."

Shifting, I drop my arm to give her some space. I've never been one for public displays of affection. In my business, you have to worry about always being photographed and some tabloid running the picture with an inaccurate click-bait type headline that most likely ends with my mother calling me to find out what's going on. With Celeste, I don't even think of those things. It's natural to touch her. Besides, we're in a New York subway. It isn't exactly like we're walking the streets of small town USA. And if my mom calls, the truth is easy to explain.

I like Celeste. A lot. And I'm going to spend as much time with her as I can until my "real life" comes calling.

"No way, mister," she scolds, lifting my arm back to her shoulder as she sighs in contentment.

Feeling like I'm ten feet tall, I relax and hold her to me as the train screeches to a halt in front of us. I step aside to let the masses exit the car, but Celeste isn't having it, she grabs my hand and drags me through the crowd like a salmon swimming upstream. We barely make it through the doors as they close.

"You've lost your big city edge, Stone. You have to be quicker than that if you want to make your train."

We stand, facing one another, holding the railing as the train jerks to life and we zip toward Manhattan. A jolt of anticipation and excitement hits me. When the train stops abruptly, Celeste stumbles forward and like the gentleman I am, I catch her.

"Hey," she whispers, looking up at me.

Instead of answering, I lean down and capture her lips with mine, my left hand gripping her waist while the right holds the metal railing as the train begins to move again. It isn't a kiss inappropriate for public but still not something I'm used to. When we separate, she burrows into my chest with a smile on her face.

Our stop comes quickly, and we bound through the doors and rush up the stairs to the street. My heart races and my mind struggles to keep up at the chaos around us. Beautiful chaos. Manhattan is like a world of its own and am honored to visit.

We begin our walk, once again holding hands. I allow Celeste to lead us, stopping for red lights and crossing at corners even before the light grants us permission. Again, not like Los Angeles at all. Then we turn and I slow my steps.

"Is it the same?"

"Yeah," I say, looking down Broadway. The productions may be different than my years trying to make it here, but the feeling is the same. You can feel the passion and drive rolling out of the crevices of each building.

"Do you miss it?"

Turning to face Celeste, and with complete honesty, I say, "More than I realized."

We stroll down Broadway as Celeste regales me with her dreams of working on a major production. An aspiration I share. Sure, big budget action flicks are cool and working on a popular television show has its perks, but I haven't given up my dream of one day returning to the stage. Maybe I'll be like Daniel Radcliffe or Mark Ruffalo and make a splash on Broadway.

"Shit!" Celeste exclaims, holding her phone in my face.

I'm not sure what I'm looking at, so I don't respond but she does it for me. "I have to be at the rehearsal space in twenty minutes. We need to boogie, Stone."

"Lead the way," I direct as if it's necessary. My little firecracker is on a mission and while my stride may be longer, she's fast, that's for sure.

She bobs and weaves through the foot traffic and in no time, we're standing in front of a non-descript building with a glass door. The same door with a handwritten note that reads "No public restroom here. Don't ask." Well, okay then.

Releasing my hand, Celeste shakes her hands beside her body then moves her neck. If I'm not mistaken, she's bouncing on the balls of her feet. Is she going into the ring to box or to work? At this point I'm not sure.

Taking a deep breath that she holds for a few beats before exhaling, she grabs the handle of the door and pulls. Going nowhere. That's a little bit of a letdown after the lead up.

"Dammit."

Pulling out her phone, she lifts it to her ear and says, "Hi. Yes, I know the time. No I'm not late. But I will be if someone doesn't open the door. Oh. Got it."

Tossing the phone in her bag, she turns to me. "Apparently we're the only ones here today. There's a door in the alley. Come on."

Once we've entered the building, I laugh to myself. I think I may have actually had one of my performances at this place back in my day. Or maybe it's just similar to the small startups I spent too many months working at.

I step aside, keeping myself in the shadows as a portly man greets Celeste. He's loud and boisterous and very excited to see my girl. She seems equally as thrilled as she giggles and smacks him in the arm. He pokes his head around her, spotting me against the wall. His eyes narrow as he assesses me. I wait for him to recognize me, but the time never comes.

Celeste turns to see what he's looking at and gives me the sweetest smile. Stepping forward, I don't say anything but accept the hand she's extended.

"Manuel, this is my friend. Thank you for letting him hang out for a bit."

"It's a small price to pay for you to save me from working with that she-devil. Hello, I'm Manuel Hernandez and you are…"

With his hand extended, he pauses, inviting me to introduce myself. "It's nice to meet you. I'm …" I don't say my name but turn to face Celeste. We didn't talk about telling anyone I was in town or coming here. I'd rather not have word get out, but I also have manners.

"Manuel, you have to promise not to say anything. Do not shout. Do not freak out. And whatever you do, do not tell anyone."

Furrowing his brow, Manuel looks to Celeste, never letting go of my hand. "It's nice to meet you, Manuel. I'm Hunter Stone."

Barking out a laugh, he releases my hand and smacks me on the arm. "Hilarious. And I'm Sir Anthony Hopkins."

Removing my hat I wait for him to stop laughing and realize I'm being truthful. Instead, he goes on. And on. And on. I'm not sure if I should be offended he doesn't believe I'm me or if I should remember how great this unshaved look works to keep myself unrecognizable.

"It's true. This is my friend, Hunter. He's in town for a few days and trying to keep a low profile. How likely is it that nobody will notice him?"

Stopping mid laugh, Manuel rights himself and takes a deep breath. "Holy shit. Hunter Stone. Wow. It's nice to meet you. My kids are huge fans of your show. I can't say anyone will recognize you. How about a pseudonym? Is there something we can call you? Maybe your real name?"

Laughing, "Hunter is my real name."

"Really? It sounds so…"

"Hollywood?" I ask, and he nods sheepishly. "Yeah, I know. How about Daniel? It's my dad's name."

With that decided, Manuel turns toward the stage and pauses. "How would you feel about helping us with some blocking? It's just the initial crew here and it would help if Celeste and I didn't have to fill in."

"I can do that."

With a smack on my shoulder, Manuel leads us across the large room. Like I did in the tropics with Celeste, I feel more relaxed than I have in years.

Chapter 16

Celeste

It's an odd feeling when you become friends with someone you admire. Or in my case when you start sleeping with your celebrity crush.

On the one hand, Hunter is just a man. A sweet, shy, generous man with dreams and aspirations I can relate to. In the short time we've known each other, I've realized how much we have in common. Not only our love of theater and New York. We both like to sit in quiet while we read and not be distracted by music. Funfetti cake is superior regardless of what others say. And, we both like to snuggle and talk into the late hours with only the moonlight guiding us. Those late night conversations are my favorite.

Then randomly, I will have a weird moment where I want to fangirl over "Hunter Stone" the television and now movie star of my dreams sitting next to me. I freely admit, watching him assisting Manuel with blocking ideas and getting into character as he read from a script was one of those moments. I was supposed to be getting to know the crew and taking measurements for set design while he assisted Manuel. Instead, I got lost watching Hunter work.

He was larger than life. Larger than that stage. And I was reminded once again how very different our lives are and for good reason. I have yet to find my footing in this industry while he continued to flourish. His talent and ease were apparent, and I couldn't stop myself from watching.

I also couldn't help the smile that came over me as I did. Thoughts of how lucky I am that he has chosen to spend his time with me. Plus the sex. Woowee the sex is off the charts.

Now that we're back at my place, the movie star has once again disappeared, replaced by the regular everyday man who is perched in the corner of our small couch, his feet on my thrift store coffee table while he absentmindedly scrolls through his text messages and scratches his balls. I don't even think he knows he's doing it.

Yep. Just a regular guy. A super-hot regular guy I wouldn't mind having here forever but a regular guy, nonetheless.

I'm tucked up on the other side of the couch, reading through my new script and making notes to go over with Manuel tomorrow. We spent six hours at work today with me playing catch-up and Manuel trying to keep things on schedule. There is so much to do if we're trying to open in the next couple of months.

I nudge Hunter with my foot. "Not avoiding your phone anymore?"

He sighs deeply and turns to look at me, releasing his nuts and grabbing my leg instead, stroking it gently. "I figured I should at least let my mother know I'm not dead."

"You've been scrolling for a while. She really leave you that many messages?"

He laughs once. "She left me one asking me to call her when I get home, so she knows I made it back okay. But then I saw the millions of messages left by my manager and decided to read them. Bad idea."

I grimace. "Is he pissed you're still here?"

"He doesn't know. At least I haven't told him where I am. I'm not to the end of the messages yet. So far it's mostly updates on scheduling changes. According to the message left on"—he looks at his phone again—"Monday, there's been a delay in production."

"That's good, right? It gives you more time?"

"No idea. That may have changed in the last couple days. I need to keep scrolling to confirm."

I give him that look, the one all women give when they think their man needs to stop avoiding and face something head on. Not that he's my man, per se, but we've been playing the role for close to a week, so I think it's safe to pretend it to be true.

"Hunter," I say gently. "Maybe you should just call him and get it over with."

He drops his head onto the back of the couch and blows out a breath. Apparently the dramatics aren't only for the small screen. "I know. I'm just not ready to go back."

"So don't," I say with a shrug. "Tell him up front you need some more time to rest and then talk through whatever scheduling he has. Need his contact info? I have it right here." I grab the small binder off the table that has my important lists and several business cards I may need. Pulling Eddie's out, I wave it playfully Hunter's direction. "Some random guy gave it to me, but I'll share with you."

"Let me see that." With a smile, Hunter grabs it out of my hand. "Some guy," he grumbles with an eyeroll. The memory of him giving me that card is in the forefront of my mind and I wonder if it is in his too. As he looks, his face falls. "Wait a minute."

I watch curiously as he opens his phone once again and begins searching for something. Then he laughs humorlessly, and I know he's found what he's looking for.

"Mystery solved."

"What are you talking about?"

"The response you never got about the interview. You sent the email to the wrong address."

Furrowing my brow, I know that can't be true. "I triple checked that address. Probably quadruple checked before I sent it."

"Oh I have no doubt. But Eddie is an idiot who thinks raised ink on his business cards makes him look fancy. Instead, it made the dot between his first and last name rub off."

"Give me that." I snatch the card back out of his hand and sure enough, there is no dot between names. "So this whole time I thought Eddie was just ignoring me when really some other random guy got my email."

Hunter nods slowly. "It seems that way. Makes me wonder how many opportunities I've missed because of this damn card. Also makes me wonder who keeps getting the messages and what he thinks."

With a vigor he hasn't had when it comes to his Samsung since, well, not ever that I've seen, he opens it once again and dials. It doesn't take long for the tongue-lashing to begin. "Eddie… yeah it's me. Yes, I'm fine. No I haven't been kidnapped. Eddie… Eddie… stop talking, Eddie, and listen for a second. You need to get some new business cards."

I can't help my giggle. Of all things to finally motivate Hunter to get back to life, it's a missing dot.

"I told you the raised ink was a bad idea. No… Yes… I'm looking at the card right here. There's no dot…"

I tune out their conversation and get back to my note taking. The script is good and entertaining. Not that there is any question since it's been picked up by a production company. Regardless, my eyes wander to the table where my own unfinished screenplay sits. I can't figure out why the story isn't coming together, nor can I figure out why I have no interest in figuring it out. I haven't touched it since the flight to the wedding. Even then, I spent most of the time correcting my punctuation more than anything. Writer's block is a terrible thing. I don't know how authors do it.

No matter. The screenplay is a dream and I have a job to do. The stage can't manage itself.

Hunter continues his call with Eddie. I'm only half listening while he discusses scheduling and photo shoots and a bunch of stuff I don't really understand. When he finally hangs up and tosses his phone on the table, I put the script down and turn my attention to him.

"Got it all sorted out?"

"Yeah." He goes back to rubbing my leg absent-mindedly. The feeling gives me goose bumps he doesn't seem to notice. "Unless something comes up, it looks like I have a few more weeks to rest up. Maybe hang out a bit?"

I can see the question in his eyes. The wonder if he's imposing on my life. The answer is a resounding no. Not just for my purposes, but I feel like he needs to stay here for a while as well. Call it woman's intuition, but he seemed so free while he lost himself in character last night. I just know helping out for a while will give him the mental rest he desperately needs.

"How do you feel about hanging out with me at work for a couple of days? Share some of that big shot actor knowledge with Manuel."

Hunter's eyes light up. "Yeah?"

"Of course."

His smile is contagious. Or maybe it's the excitement in his eyes. At least I think it's excitement. Hunter turns to me, eyes glazed, as he slowly moves so he's over my body and up the couch.

"I'm not an inconvenience in your apartment?"

Tossing my script aside, I scooch my butt so I'm lying down underneath him. "Not even close. Besides," I say, running my fingers through his hair. "I already told you I'm not kicking you out of my bed any time soon."

"What about your couch?" he asks as he positions himself between my legs.

"You're safe on my couch too."

He shifts his hips, sending shockwaves through my entire body. "What about your life?"

His movement combined with his words makes me gasp, my heart doing a staccato as I process his words. "How long and how much you are in my life is totally up to you."

Hunter smiles shyly and finally leans down to seal our conversation with a kiss. A kiss that's long, languished… and interrupted when Anna walks in the door.

"Honey, I'm home… oh. Well. Looks like you

were getting to home too, weren't ya, Fluffy?"

Hunter collapses on me with a groan as I giggle at the interruption. And the nickname. Of course the one week I have limited time with Hunter, Anna's dog walker job is cancelled. Something about the agency she works for having to discuss the "lack of appropriate boundaries" by their pet. I don't understand it since every dog I've ever known stuck its nose in my crotch, but it makes no difference. All I need to know is Anna has been in and out more than normal lately, and it's not a good idea to get naked on the couch because of it.

"What are you doing home?" I ask and push Hunter off me. He goes back to the opposite side of the couch, albeit reluctantly, his hair sticking up in an unruly mess.

Anna grabs her new box of Twinkies and rips into one, sighing as she chews before talking around her bite. "The subway was kind of dead. People were really stingy with their tip money and I got bored. Figured I'd get a good night's sleep and go out again tomorrow. I've got some new music I'd like to try out. See what kind of response I get."

"Just don't forget we need your blog post. I need to update that in a couple days."

Anna snaps her fingers together like she just remembered, not that I reminded her. "That's right. I've already listened to Denise Pugotti's new album. It's really good. Think we can have a couple sample bites on the post?"

"Sure," I say with a shrug. "We've never done it before but anything interesting to get subscribers to come back just increases our ability to get ad revenue."

She gives me a thumbs up and crams the last bit of plastic-y goodness in her mouth. "Sounds good. I'm headed to my room so you two can get back to whatever I interrupted. I'll make sure to wear my headphones."

Hunter blushes at her matter-of-factness, which I find endearing. As confident as he is in his craft, I notice he is a little shyer when it comes to discussing personal things. Or perhaps it's just my roommate's directness that makes him come off as shy. Regardless, it balances my bluntness and I like having that in my life.

Not that I should be thinking that way. What we have is a weekend fling with an extension. Nothing more.

So why does my heart seem to have missed the memo?

Chapter 17

Hunter

"I feel bad. Are you sure you'll be okay?" Her big eyes are wide with concern.

"Celeste, I promise it's fine. I'm supposed to be on a sabbatical, remember? That means lounging on your couch eating and napping is completely acceptable."

We've been having this conversation for the last twenty minutes and while I appreciate her being worried about my well-being, I hate that she feels any sort of guilt. I'm the one who should be apologizing for even making her feel that way. I've intruded on her life and it isn't her responsibility to take care of me. Although, I will admit I kind of love it. It's nice that she cares so much about something as menial as if I can entertain myself for a few hours. Then again, she may be more concerned I'll drug myself again or unknowingly eat another of Anna's precious snacks. Both scenarios could end with pictures of me trending all across social media. Maybe she should be concerned.

Scrunching her face, Celeste eyeballs my snack of choice. She leans over and I ignore the way my heart rate speeds up as she comes within inches of my face. That's what she does to me. This wild-haired beauty who makes me feel more like myself than I have in ages. I know when her lips land on mine…

"Hey! Get your hands off my Ding Dong!"

"That's not what you said this morning," she sasses as she takes a bite of the chocolate covered cake.

Once Anna mentioned them the other day, I made Celeste stop at the market on the corner for a supply. I grabbed two boxes—one for me and one as a peace offering for Anna. I should have gotten more. I'll make sure to add that to my shopping list. Thank goodness for at home delivery. I can have this place stocked by the time she gets home from her meeting.

This time when Celeste leans forward, her lips land on mine and I pull her into my lap. Her giggles are muffled by my lips as I taste the chocolate on her tongue. How long has it been since I've been this relaxed? So carefree and uninhibited? I can't even remember it's been so long. How pathetic.

"I better go if I'm going to make it on time. Enjoy your mindless television and snacks. I'll text you when I'm on my way home."

She lifts off my lap, giving me a full glimpse of her

glorious behind and I smack it for good measure. The gesture makes her jump and then stumble. Whoops. The glare she gives me is meant to be intimidating but it only makes me smile.

Before Celeste can make it to the front door, there are three quick raps. Lifting to her toes, she looks through the peep hole before opening the door. I watch from my spot on the couch and hear her thank the person before closing the door.

"Well, so much for your day of leisure," she remarks as she walks my way, her arms carrying a box.

I accept the package from her and set it on the table before ripping off the tape and peering inside. Damn Eddie and his demand I make this a working sabbatical.

"Dang," Celeste says as she peers it the box. "Eddie doesn't mess around. That has to be at least six scripts."

"I know. I won't read them all. If by the first forty pages or so I'm not interested I'll set it aside and move on to the next. Now go. I'll see you later."

Groaning, she doesn't argue and rushes toward the door. When it closes, I lean back on the couch and exhale. Alone. I'm all alone. Nowhere to be and nobody to meet. It's been months since I've had an entire day with no plans like this. I should just focus on the manuscripts Eddie shipped and get that out of the way.

Opening the box, I lift out the first submission and settle in for what may be my next movie. I've never told Eddie this, but I don't only read the scripts for acting roles but also potential producing opportunities. I love bringing characters to life and pushing my acting limits but ultimately I would like to spend more time behind the scenes. Not necessarily movies. I think I'd prefer producing plays or musicals. I definitely don't think that directing is something I would enjoy since I can barely tell Eddie what to do let alone a cast of actors but producing has always interested me.

Before I begin, though, I need to order groceries. As much as I enjoy snack cakes, I need some real food as well.

Hours tick by. Groceries have been ordered and scripts have been perused. Some of the scripts have interested me. There's one adaptation of a romance novel that I was surprised made it into the box, but I liked the premise, and it would be something different than people expect of me. My eyes and mind need a break. Checking my online order, I confirm the groceries I've ordered won't deliver for a few more hours. Thankfully, pizza is a different story.

Scrolling through my phone, I skim a few reviews of local pizza places and choose one that has a high star rating and a lot of "THE BEST PIZZA EVER" titles. The all capitals is what caught my attention. Once my order is complete, I toss my phone aside and pick up the remote for the television. Some of that mindless television Celeste mentioned sounds great.

The thing about acting on television is I don't watch it often. The last thing I need to do is happen across

Prince of Darkness and see myself on the screen. I shudder at the thought. Oh geez, I wonder if my mom watches the show? I mean I know she watches but does she *watch*. We may be on one of the top five major television networks, but our directors like to push the limits. We are a vampire show and everyone knows vampires are virile bloodsuckers.

Not wanting to take a chance, I pull up the ladies' DVR and sort through the list. My phone rings next to me and I see Celeste's name on the screen. Abandoning my search, I pick up the call.

"Miss me?"

"Terribly," she sasses.

I won't tell her I miss her. I don't want to be the guy that guilts a professional woman into even contemplating cutting her day short because I selfishly want her sitting on this couch next to me. I've grown quite accustomed to spending my time with Celeste.

"We're on a quick break so I thought I'd see what you were up to."

"Oh you know, searching the medicine cabinet, riffling through your drawers. Why haven't I seen that black lacy number hidden in the back of your sock drawer?"

She snorts a laugh which makes me smile. "Nice try. I don't have a sock drawer."

Kicking my feet up on the table, I settle in for a little flirtation. "But you do have a black lacy number?"

"Perhaps. What are you up to?"

"Just waiting on my lunch to be delivered."

A door closes in the background and the line is a little muffled before I hear traffic in the background.

"Are you outside?"

"Yeah, I needed a little fresh air. Want to grab a late dinner? Maybe a slice of pizza?"

"How about I treat you to sushi?"

"Mr. Stone, are you trying to romance me into bed? You know I'm a sure thing."

I love her humor and sass. Damn do I love it. "Romance in the form of a poké roll."

We chat a few minutes longer before Celeste is called back into rehearsal and my pizza arrives. I'm all about conservation so I don't bother with a plate. The provided napkins will work just fine. Folding the pizza in half like a taco, my mouth waters as I lift the slice to my mouth. A burst of flavor hits my taste buds. Delicious.

Resuming my search of something to watch, I hold the slice in one hand and the remote in the other. Then I see it. Choking on my pizza, I toss it in the box and wipe my face with a napkin before taking a drink of my water.

"Oh Celeste. What do we have here?"

Season 1. Season 2. Season 3.

All three seasons of Prince of Darkness. All recorded. I remember asking her the other night as we lay in her bed talking about a specific storyline. She insisted she had only seen a few episodes and couldn't really remember the storylines. I am going to make so much fun of her. I doubt she lied for any nefarious reasons, but it's going to be fun finding out the truth.

Since the last thing I want to do is watch myself, I exit the DVR list and settle on a true crime documentary. It's six episodes and should be enough for me to distract myself until I meet my girl for dinner and a show. Because I plan to tease her enough to entertain myself the entire meal.

"Come on, babe, don't be pissed. I was just kidding."

Whipping around to stare me down, she narrows her eyes and points her finger. "Don't babe me. Nicknames and that… that sexiness is not going to distract me from being angry."

Sauntering up to her, I slip my hands around her waist and tug her flush to me. "You think I'm sexy?"

"Ugh! Hunter stop!"

Waggling my eyebrows, I move my hips and cup her ass in my hands. "I'm sorry. I was just teasing you. You love Prince of Darkness. It's great. As an actor on the show, I thank you."

"Love is a little strong."

As she says the words a fleeting thought of what could be hits me, but it's gone just as quickly. We barely know one another. Yes, I love spending time with her. She makes me laugh and feel more like myself than anyone else. I care for her. A lot. But hearing her use the word love has me suddenly longing for more.

"I'm wounded. Are you saying you don't love the show that has made me a household name?"

"Fine. Maybe I thought it was ridiculous and I needed to see what the hype was all about. Then some hunky guy strutted across the screen and piqued my interest."

"Oh hunky guy, you say? Does he happen to look like a lumberjack?"

"Nah, he's this Viking looking guy with an accent. It's the accent that gets me every time."

Dropping my jaw, I gasp at the audacity of her giving so much credit to my co-star. "Blasphemy!"

"Actually he says bollocks a lot."

I release my hold on her and step back, scoffing and placing my hands on my hips in offense. Now it's her turn to laugh and smirk.

"I'm kidding. Yes, Hunter Stone, you are the only reason I watch that damn show. If you tell anyone I will cut you off from sex for the rest of your life."

Again that thought of what could be, zips through my mind. Celeste smiles and rises on her toes, placing a kiss to my lips. "I'm kidding. That would suck for me."

Spinning on her heel, Celeste struts away, giggling

the entire way to the couch. Slumping onto the couch, she kicks her feet up on the table and pats the spot next to her. When I assume the spot indicated, she cuddles into my side and takes my hand in hers.

"Really, I never planned to watch Prince of Darkness. I didn't even have a TV. But when I knew you snagged a spot as a regular cast member, I had to check it out. While it doesn't make sense, I was proud of you." She fidgets with my hand, rubbing circles on my palm, not making eye contact with me. "Knowing how far you'd come and how hard you worked to get there... I don't know, I was happy to see you making it."

Placing a kiss on the top of her head I say, "Thank you. I was proud of me too. I wish I knew you then. To have you share that with me. At the time, my family was proud. My dad and mom telling everyone they knew about their son the actor. There were so few people in my life that I trusted in the industry it would have been nice to have someone who understood how big of a deal it was."

"Tell me about your family."

"They're the best. My parents have been married thirty-two years and still love one another. I have two sisters and a brother. My extended family is a little complicated. My dad's side is loud and crazy while my mom's is a little more traditional."

"What was it like growing up in an interracial family? Or do you call it multi-cultural?"

Chuckling at her question, I think back to my

childhood before I respond. "Would you believe me if I never thought about it? Actually, would you believe I didn't realize we were an interracial or multi-cultural family until I was in my twenties?"

Jumping up, she almost whacks my chin with her head as she spins to face me, eyes wide. "What?"

Shrugging I say, "It's embarrassing to admit but it's true. We didn't grow up focusing on race or culture. My mom's side of the family is Hispanic and my dad's… I don't know, he checks the white box when necessary. There's some Native American and a lot of European descent too. My mom's mom passed when I was young and after that the traditions died out. In the end, we were just the Stones. We have a big family and it's loud and crazy but full of love. It wasn't until someone mentioned it to me in my twenties that I realized there was a time my parents weren't supposed to be together. That they were looked at differently. For us kids, we were just us."

"That's pretty cool," Celeste comments as she settles back into my side. "Your family sounds great."

I don't tell her I can't wait for her to meet them. That may be moving a little fast for whatever it is we're doing.

Chapter 18

Celeste

I look down at my phone and fight back my grin as I answer. "Yes, Manuel. What can I help you with?"

I left rehearsal less than thirty minutes ago after a long day of scheduling meetings, contacting acting schools to give them audition information, going over set design ideas—there is a lot to do at this stage of production and still no guarantees the producer will green light it to the stage. A fact that Manuel seems to be taking to heart with how much he focuses on getting things rolling. Based on the number of texts I get every night, I'm not sure he sleeps anymore.

"I want to see if you've started advertising for auditions yet."

It's a valid question. We discussed just about everything else but got distracted when one of the producers showed up unannounced, so auditions is the one thing we never talked about.

"Yep," I say as I dodge the foot traffic around me as I walk. "It's listed on the normal sites—Backstage, Playbill, a couple other places I have written down. I reached out to the head of a few acting schools in case they have any up and coming talent we don't want to miss. Social media is updated. I think there's more but I'm fresh off the subway and hoofing it home."

"Great. Sounds like you've got everything covered. I don't want us to take this casting lightly."

"Agreed."

The play we're working on, "The Dreamer" is set in a small mining town in the 1940s. Our main character is having an existential crisis as he aspires to make a difference in his community by moving into politics. His family doesn't agree. It's a beautiful coming of age story based on the real life issues from that era. It also means period costumes, fascinating sets, and a world most of us weren't alive for and will never experience except through the theater. It's wonderful.

"I'll check my email when I get home in case I have a response from any of the schools yet," I add. "But since it's after hours I doubt there will be anything."

"Text me one way or the other."

"Will do." Approaching my building, I grab my key to unlock the front door. "I'm almost home so you'll hear from me in a couple hours at the most."

"Cool. Thanks, Celeste. I knew you and I would have the same vision for this one."

We hang up and I shove my phone in my back pocket, not somewhere I'd normally keep it while walking down the street, but this is my hallway. My neighbors would be stupid to try and pickpocket me since I know where they live.

As soon as my door opens, I'm overcome by the most amazing aroma that makes my stomach growl immediately. Dropping my keys into a bowl by the door, I only have to take a couple steps before I find the source of the great scents.

"Are you making dinner?"

Hunter looks over his shoulder and smiles at me. Not the movie star smile, but the one I only get to see when we're alone.

"Hey. I hope you're hungry. I'm making salmon tacos."

I drop onto a bar stool and notice the counter is covered with all the fixings for soft tacos, including sautéed orange and yellow peppers, guacamole, and what looks like homemade salsa. But even the food doesn't distract me from the show in front of me. I can't help it as I watch Hunter's back shift and flex through his T-shirt. With the possible exception of a man with a baby, there is nothing sexier than a man making his woman dinner. Not that I'm necessarily his woman but I sure wouldn't mind if I was. Hunter Stone is quickly and efficiently burrowing his way into my everyday thoughts.

"Salmon, huh? I feel kind of fancy eating the expensive fish," I joke. "Tilapia is more in my budget." No, actually it's not. Shrimp flavored Ramen is about as good as it gets around here.

Transferring the now shredded fish into a bowl, Hunter turns and deposits it onto the island. "As much as I'm enjoying eating my weight in snacks of my childhood, I need to get back on track with my eating habits. Besides, I figured the least I could do is make you a home-cooked meal since you've been housing and entertaining me."

"It is much appreciated. Manuel sprung for sandwiches today, but they weren't very good. Definitely not as good-looking as this spread."

Like the gentleman he is, Hunter hands me a plate to go first. "Dig in."

He doesn't have to tell me twice. I waste no timing filling my tortillas high with salmon, rice, peppers, guac, and salsa. It smells so good, my mouth waters, and when I lick a drop of salsa off my thumb, I groan with satisfaction.

Hunter makes a choking sound which has me looking up and realizing I accidentally made a sex noise. Giggling, I shrug. "Oopsie."

Hunter just shakes his head and fills his own plate full of food.

As we eat, he questions me about the show—when auditions are, what Manuel's vision for casting is, and the tentative timeline. He's so much more invested in this play than I anticipated, and it makes me feel good. Like my passion is more than just mine. I like sharing it with him.

On the flip side, he tells me about the one script he seems interested in looking into further—a romantic comedy that is like nothing he's ever done before but would be a nice change of pace and would show more of his range. No actor wants to end up typecast. Of course no actor's girlfriend likes the idea of her boyfriend as the man who does all the kissing in a movie.

Not that he's my boyfriend. Or I'm his girlfriend. Or that we're even in a relationship.

Hell, I don't know what exactly we're doing right now but the longer it continues, the more I enjoy it and don't want it to end. We may only be playing like we're together, but I'll pretend as long as he wants. It's still more fulfilling and easier than any "real" relationship I've ever been part of.

"Can I ask you a question?"

I lick the juices off my finger and realize I'm shoveling this food in my face like I've never eaten before. Super sexy, Celeste.

"Sure."

"What's the script you're writing?"

I pause. The one thing that could distract me from the best dinner I've had since, well since we went to that little dinette, is conversation about my writer's block.

I finish chewing and swallow, slowly wiping my hands with a napkin. "In my mind, it's a fantastic movie script that some producer will snatch up and turn into a blockbuster."

Hunter smirks. We both know it's not that simple. "And in reality?"

I let out a heavy sigh. "It's the unfinished piece of crap I've been working on for a couple years that I can't make heads nor tails of and I can't figure out the problem."

Hunter pushes his plate away and leans on his forearms. "Maybe you're stuck because your passion is plays over movies."

I have had that thought before, but the dynamics of the characters seem hard to translate to stage versus screen. At this point, with it being not much more than an outline, it feels very intimate talking about the project.

"Maybe," is the only response I give feeling slightly uncomfortable knowing he found it and there's a possibility he may have read it. No one's done that before. Not even Anna. But she's also a musician and doesn't like people reading her songs before their done so she understands the need for privacy with my words.

Hunters warm palm covers my hand and he squeezes. "I'm sorry. I didn't intend to snoop. It got mixed up with the scripts I was tossing on the table. That's the only reason I picked it up. I thought I'd missed something Eddie sent."

The look in his eyes shows true remorse for accidentally invading my private creativity. How can I be angry when he looks like that?

"I know. And I appreciate your take on it. Who knows, maybe I'll switch it to a play and my brain will unlock itself because of it."

"Maybe so. But for now, concentrate on dinner. We don't want that salmon to go to waste."

"Oh believe me, it won't," I say, taking another huge bite.

After inhaling three tacos, I take a deep breath, willing my stomach to expand just a little. "Why am I always stuffing myself when we eat together?"

He shrugs. "Maybe it's because you know I like feeding you."

"Because it makes you feel dominant over little old me?" I joke and nudge his shoulder.

"No," he says as he picks up his plate and walks to the sink. "Because I have very vivid memories of being a starving artist, and I like knowing I'm doing my part to help you reach your dreams. Even if it's just making sure you eat something not full of MSG every once in a while."

Oh look. See that puddle of goo on the floor? That's me, because I just completely melted at those words.

"You're a good man, Hunter Stone."

"You're a good woman, Celeste Pumper-whatever-er." He leans over the island as I stand up and meet him halfway for a blood-pumping kiss that ends too soon when his phone rings.

"Dammit," he grumbles and grabs it to see who so rudely interrupted what was shaping up to be a very fulfilling evening. "It's Eddie. Probably wants to know about the scripts. Give me a minute?"

"Sure. You cooked. It's only fair that I clean."

He rounds the corner and gives me a quick peck before walking into the living room. "Hey, Eddie, what's up?"

I make quick work of dishing out meal-sized servings into my fancy storage containers, also known as old butter and yogurt containers. There's a small fridge in our rehearsal space so I'll be taking this goodness for lunch tomorrow. I have no guilt whatsoever about leaving only a little for Hunter to have.

Once that's done, I get to tackle my least favorite part—the creation of dishpan hands. Anna and I had a choice—higher rent with a dishwasher or washing by hand. We chose Palmolive. At this point, I'm used to it from doing it for so long, but I swear Hunter used every single pot and pan we own. Not that there are many. We don't exactly have much kitchen storage space. But it still takes some time and effort to get it all done. I'm not bothered by it. It just gives Hunter time to converse with his manager without feeling like I'm hovering.

As I finally finish up, I turn and wipe my hands dry on a tea towel. It appears my timing is perfect, and

Hunter is done with his call. Or at least he's no longer listening because he's holding the phone in his hands and staring down at it.

"Hey." I hang the towel on the drawer pull. "Everything okay?"

He looks up at me, sadness in his eyes. "Um… I have to go back to L.A."

I feel a chill as my heart plummets. "When?" I ask quietly, afraid my voice will break.

He swallows hard before answering me. "Tomorrow morning. Eddie's booking my flight now."

And just like that, our little bubble of passion for the theater and each other has popped. I've never hated his job more.

Chapter 19

Hunter

I know I'm being a moody jerk. My level of care is somewhere between "don't give a shit" and "really don't give a shit." Okay that's not true, I do care. Just not enough to not grumble at every comment and direction.

My integrity and strong work ethic are both traits I inherited from my parents and I'm proud of myself for maintaining them as I maneuver through this industry. Yet, the expectation for me to jump from weeks of time with Celeste in New York, resting and relaxing, to not seeing her and being expected to put on a happy face while my job goes full speed ahead is a little much.

Photo shoots have never bothered me, and it's an honor to be chosen for this cover as one of the hottest actors under thirty. I'm barely making the cut, but I'll take it even if thirty is just a blink away. When I answered Eddie's call two days ago and he rambled on about publicity and opportunities, I didn't hear a thing he said. To me it was all white noise once he uttered the words "We need you home asap."

Not because I didn't know the call would come but because the word "home" seemed so foreign to me. The thought of my condo in L.A. no longer held the standard for a home like the small apartment Celeste and Anna shared. My place was decorated by a designer friend of a friend of Eddie's while the apartment in New York was full of life. Each piece of furniture and décor told a story. Even the television Celeste bought so she could watch me. That one was my favorite.

"Hunter, drop your chin a little for me."

Doing as instructed, I shift slightly and clear my mind and focus on the task at hand. I'm in my third wardrobe change and I don't even have to ask, I know the photographer has his shot. It was the first one of this series. When I looked up at his direction and saw a blonde walking in the distance. I thought briefly that it was Celeste. That she decided to surprise me.

It wasn't. Nah, it was a dude who is in a Twisted Sister cover band and was dropping off a package on his way to a gig. Disappointment was what I felt but the guy snapping the frames called it "haunting and real." Whatever.

"That's a wrap on Hunter Stone."

Stepping down from the stool I'm perched on, I

accept the light applause and accolades as I move to the wardrobe area. Applause and congratulations for having my picture taken. This industry is weird.

"Mr. Stone, if you'll just leave those clothes on the bench behind the screen, I'll make sure to get everything put away."

"No problem, Dina. Let me clean this makeup off and I'll get changed."

She smiles at me and the way the lines around her eyes crinkle, she reminds me of my mom. Speaking of, I need to call her back and accept her invitation to Sunday dinner. It's been months since I've seen my family and, while we stay connected via text message and the occasional Facetime, I miss them.

Now that the vacation beard is gone, it only takes a minute to successfully remove the makeup used to even out my skin tone and give me that "natural look." Yeah, I get the irony too. Exchanging my cover model costume for my regular clothes, I step from behind the screen used to create a dressing area and find Eddie waiting for me, his nose buried in his phone as his fingers fly across the screen.

"Ya ready?" he asks, never looking up.

"Sure. Are you positive I have to go to this thing? I'm exhausted and haven't even unpacked my luggage."

Turning, he doesn't respond immediately, so I follow him like a dutiful puppy. The car service is waiting for us as we exit the building. Ducking into the back seat, I wait for him to finish his manic typing and turn to me. I'm used to this side of Eddie and while it doesn't usually bother me, I'd like an answer to my question. Preferably one where he says no, I don't have to slip into celebrity mode and dazzle the cameras.

Eddie turns to face me. "I know premieres aren't your favorite, which is why I declined the last two to give you the time off you requested. But, this is an opening of a new club and the other hot-under-thirty celebs will be there. You've fallen off the radar the last few weeks and we need to get you visible again."

"I get it. I just wish I didn't have to do these things. It was nice being just a person for a while."

His phone vibrates, pulling his attention away from our conversation. Taking his cue, I bring my own device to life and scroll the texts looking for one from Celeste. She hasn't sent anything since her response to me this morning. Well, my morning and her afternoon. It's close to the time she usually leaves rehearsal, so I tap out a quick text.

Me: How was rehearsal?

I'm not surprised she doesn't reply immediately. It isn't like she's just hanging out waiting for my text. After a few minutes, the three dots begin to bounce, and I relax into the leather of the seat.

Celeste: Ongoing...

Me: It's late. Did you take a long lunch or something?

Celeste: Nah. We coordinated the

schedule for auditions next week
and then Manuel had "a vision." So
here I am. Me and a cold slice of
pizza.

Me: I could go for a slice of NY
pizza.

Celeste: I miss you eating NY pizza.

My chuckle startles Eddie and he shoots me a glare.
Ignoring him, I read her next text.

Celeste: I made it weird, didn't I?
Pretend I didn't say that. How's
the weather? What are you doing?

Me: Just finished a shoot for that
article and going home to change.
I have to do some sort of club
opening.

Celeste: Crap I have to go. Call me
later. My later not yours. Xo

"That the girl?" Eddie asks, motioning to my
phone.

"If by girl you mean Celeste, yes. By the way did
you order new business cards? If I've missed out on an
award-winning role because of that damn dot I'll haunt
you from the afterlife."

"Yes, I ordered new cards. You know that you only
play a vampire on television and don't have the ability
to come back in the afterlife, right?"

"We'll see."

The drive to my condo takes longer than necessary thanks to rush hour traffic. Which, I suppose should be called simply "traffic" these days. There's no designated hour anymore. While we sit idly, barely creeping along with the other cars, Eddie rattles off the schedule for the next few weeks. How it's gone from delays upon delays to everything ramped up into hyperdrive makes me tired just thinking of it.

"I'm waiting to confirm the press junket for the new season, so we'll put a pin in that. Speaking of, the studio is waiting on us to finalize contract negotiations. Oh and yeah, there's the premiere of Sasha Ewing's new movie. It's getting a lot of Oscar buzz, so the exposure is great. I can put in a few calls for a date, just let me know brunette or redhead."

"No."

"Sorry?" he coughs out. "Did you say no? Good one, Hunter. Redhead it is."

Groaning, I roll my head back on the headrest and rub the space between my eyes, warding off a headache. Sometimes these conversations with Eddie have that effect on me. He means well and I respect his opinion. Heck, he's been in this business for over a dozen years and helped launch the careers of actors I have nothing but respect for. Yet, sometimes he doesn't hear what I tell him.

"I'm not taking a date."

"You can't possibly plan to go alone. The press will have a field day with that. No, you need to take someone."

My thoughts run through options. Celeste and I didn't talk about what happens moving forward. There was no definition of our relationship, if there even was one. Maybe she wants to leave what we had in the tropics and New York.

"How about my mom? People love that."

"Not after you've been off the radar for weeks. It has to be something to garner attention. And not the sweet mama's boy kind of attention."

"Fine," I mumble through my hand as I glide it across my face. "Penelope. She loves getting dolled up. Plus, it'll be good for us and the show. And, I don't have to worry about her trying to climb me like a tree in the limo."

Eddie claps his hands loudly, the sound echoing in the car just as we pull up in front of my building. "Excellent plan. Now, go get all hunky for the cameras, and I'll have the car pick you up in two hours."

Saluting him as I climb from the car, I laugh as his retort is a middle finger. As I enter my building, I greet Denny the security guard whose sitting behind his desk staring at the monitors, and step into the elevator for my floor. As the numbers increase on the screen, I find myself wishing for a tiny kitchen, a box of Ding Dongs, and a spunky blonde waiting for me on the other side of my door.

Chapter 20

Celeste

All is right in the world now that my small desk is organized to perfection. The everyday calendar I rely on is color coordinated based on both jobs—theater or blog, and the degree of importance. With auditions scheduled to begin soon, everything theater related is in bright, do-not-miss-this yellow. For the upcoming meeting with Carrie, I chose a pretty pink which means it's needed but not urgent and can be rescheduled if need be.

My blog calendar is also open in front of me with every upcoming review, release, and sale that we plan to heavily promote in bold letters. Lastly, emails that need to be sent are in green for "go ahead and send this."

Everything is in order, my to-do lists are updated,

and my blue notebook to jot down anything we need to tackle further is ready for this meeting. Carrie and I have spent years building and promoting this website to be the premier place to go for all your information related to anything stories—books, plays, movies, television. So why am I struggling to care?

I know why. *Hunter*.

The man showed up when I least expected him and wormed his way into my life. And if I'm being honest, my heart. Or should I say, slunk like a feline. Now, even two weeks after his rapid departure, it doesn't feel the same in this shoebox apartment without him. It feels empty.

I begin to sigh deeply when my video messenger rings, startling me and taking the relaxing breath I needed with it.

Putting on the best happy face I can muster, I click to open the screen. "Well hello there, newlywed! How was the honeymoon?"

Clearly Carrie is not putting on a front. I don't think her smile could get any wider. Married life seems to suit her well. Or maybe it's the extended trip they took. Either way, she's practically glowing.

"If you ever get a chance to go to Australia, you *must*," she insists, her eyes sparkling. "It was so much better than I imagined."

"Really?"

"Oh my gosh, yes. We spent most of our time on the coast, working our way from the Gold Coast in the north down a little past Melbourne."

I have no idea where any of that would be located on a map, but I don't ask. I can google it later if I want. I'd rather not interrupt her train of thought. Hearing her adventures sounds like a great distraction from everything else on my mind.

"Before you tell me how lucky you are to have snorkeled in what I've heard is the most beautiful place in the world, I need to know what you thought of the wildlife."

I had no idea Carrie could get more excited, but talking animals does the trick.

"The animals there are so amazing! You know how ugly possums are in the States?"

I grimace because yes, we all know those creatures are good for the earth and bad for our blood pressure when they hiss. "Yeah."

"In Australia, they look like cats!"

"Wait, what?"

"Fluffy and cute and everything. It was so weird. I saw one and thought it was like a wild cat of some sort getting ready to attack the poor penguins as they left the ocean and waddled to their burrows at night. But nope. It was a possum."

I put that in the "you learn something new every day" category in my brain. "That's… strange. Did you get to pet a kangaroo? Please say you did."

She nods vigorously and smiles. "Sure did. They

were so fun." She claps her hands together and squeals excitedly. "There's this one zoo where you can go into the kangaroo enclosure and hang out with them. I even took a selfie with one. Look."

She holds up her phone and sure enough, she and a kangaroo are just hanging out like besties. It's kind of cool, to be honest.

"You need to make that your blog profile picture."

"I know, right?" She looks down at her phone, scrolling through her memories. "Did you know kangaroos are considered pests by Aussies? Most people just hate them."

"And yet, you think they're amazing. Color me surprised."

"What does that mean?"

I appreciate my friend and her love of animals. A love I don't share. They're… fine. But too much maintenance for me.

Giggling, I remind her. "Most people in the States think squirrels are pests and yet you have one living in your house."

As if he's been summoned, her varmint jumps on her shoulder, scaring the crap out of me.

"Dammit!" I exclaim, hand to my chest. "Why does he always do that?"

Carrie begins to coo at him and hands him a nut. I find it really weird that she has random squirrel snacks just sitting on her desk, but her house, her rules.

"Uh, Carrie?"

"Uh huh?" She's not really listening to me.

"Can you maybe take him somewhere else, so he doesn't jump on your keyboard like last time? We received way too many complaints about that post he accidentally made go live."

She tsks. "People have too much time on their hands."

"It read, 'blah, blah, blah, I'll figure out how to spin this eventually.' Your friend there didn't exactly paint us in a good light."

Carrie sighs and pats his head. "He didn't mean it, but you're right. Hey, Sprite!" she yells over her non-squirrel covered shoulder. "Can you come help me for a second?"

Instead of her hilarious step-daughter, Matthew comes sauntering in the room, wiping his hands on a towel.

"Need something, babe? Hey, Celeste."

I wave as Carrie says, "Not unless you want to take Luke from me."

That stops him dead in his tracks, just as he notices the rodent sitting on her shoulder. Luke seems to notice Matthew too, turning around to face him and flipping his tail around aggressively. I think he does it on purpose because he knows Matthew is not a fan of his, as would be indicated by the giant step back he just took.

"Don't even think about it, Luke." Matthew wags

his finger at him because that's intimidating to a squirrel, I'm sure. "You stay right there. Do not come over here."

Fortunately, the little blonde cutie shows up to save the day.

"Did you call me, Carrie? Hi, Luke." Unlike her father, the child has zero fear of their weird pet and immediately begins petting him. Matthew, on the other hand, looks like he could pass out at any moment. Truly, watching the entire scene play out on my monitor is pretty damn entertaining.

"Sprite, since your daddy is a scaredy-cat, do you mind taking Luke with you so I can have my meeting?" I know the smirk on her face is at Matthew, who rolls his eyes in response.

Without hesitation, Calypso picks up the animal and cradles him to her. "Come on, Lukey Dukey. You wanna take a nap in my baby stroller again? I'll put your favorite hat on you."

And that's when I lose it, head dropping to the desk as I laugh. Calypso has a hat for the squirrel. If I didn't know these people personally, I'd think they were absolutely nuts.

"You find this funny, don't you, Celeste?" Matthew snarks, albeit playfully.

My head pops up and I wipe a stray tear from my eye. "You have the strangest family."

"Uh, excuse me," Carrie starts, and I have a feeling I'm about to get a tongue-lashing. "I don't want to hear how strange my life is when you just spent the last however long playing house with an A-list celebrity.”

“He’s not an A-lister,” I grumble, knowing full well that’s not the important part of this conversation but still feeling a little raw from his departure. “And how did you find out anyway? He was incognito and you were out of the country.”

“You forget, my new husband is a C-lister. D-lister? What would you say? E, maybe?”

Matthew holds his hands out, clearly offended. “I can hear you.”

Carrie swivels to look at him. “Well what would you say you are on the celebrity scale? If you’re anywhere close to B I wanna know when the paps are showing up to take my picture.”

He shrugs in concession. “Maybe closer to P or Q.”

Carrie turns back to me. “P it is. And as a P-list celebrity, Matthew knows celebrity gossip.”

I quirk an eyebrow because it hits me. “Eddie called when he was panicked about Hunter holing up here, didn’t he?”

Carrie waves me off dismissively. “It doesn’t matter. What’s important is that you found yourself a beau!” Her hands clap again. What is going on with her and this new giddy bouncing thing she has going?

“I would hardly call him a beau. He was here for a few days after”—I pause to choose my words because Carrie didn’t mention it, so I assume the Ambien issue hasn't made its way down the celebrity alphabet, and I should probably keep it that way—"we got back from the wedding. He made dinner, I picked up a job—it was all very low-key. No big deal."

"No big deal, huh?"

"Nope."

"Then why have we been on this call for a solid five minutes or so and you haven't started bitching at me about missing my blog deadlines yet?"

She's got me there. I'm normally chomping at the bit to stay on task. Today, my thoughts easily stray. But what she neglects to realize is she just changed the topic for me.

"Oh. My. Gosh," she says slowly. "You fell for him!"

"What?" I sit back in full denial mode. "He wasn't here long enough to fall for him. That requires months of actual dating, not a couple of weeks of hot sex."

Right? Maybe? Suddenly I don't know. Maybe that's why I feel so lost without him. Maybe I started to fall in love with him.

"I hate to tell ya, but that's not the way love works, sweetie." Carrie looks at me sympathetically, like she can read exactly how hard this is on me through the screen. I have to get us back on track. It's not that I mind her knowing how I feel. I just know me. If I dwell on it, I'll fall apart. With a new job, I don't have time to curl up in a ball on my bed and cry.

"Maybe you're right," I say with more vigor than I feel. "But right now we have limited time so let's get back to work. I was meaning to tell you, Anna's idea of audio sample worked so well we've seen a spike in activity on the music page."

"Oh that's great!"

Good. It worked. She's been distracted and I can try to concentrate on business instead of the Ding Dongs I found in the cabinet this morning.

"It gets better," I add. "She accidentally secured an ad for us with one of the small record labels she's been chatting with. They want to run a two-week promotion for an album they're trying to get buzz about."

Carrie looks delighted by this news. Or maybe she's still sated from the honeymoon. Regardless, this is fantastic all the way around. "It was such a good idea to add Anna to the mix."

"She's turning into a bigger asset than I anticipated." I jot down a note to find out when Anna wants to run her own ad. For a couple blog posts on the music scene every month, she bartered for some promo of her own music. I don't want to forget that. "That's all I have on advertisers. Everything else is the same. How's it going on your end? Get some books read and reviewed on your trip?"

"Not many," she says with a waggle of her eyebrows as I groan. I swear, when that girl finally cut off her chastity belt, Matthew didn't stand a chance. "Don't worry. I have what we need. But I also have an exclusive interview."

This grabs my attention. "Meaning?"

"Okay, you know how I'm friends with Donna Moreno?"

"Super erotica romance writing author who suddenly broke out into sweet romance? I've heard you mention her a time or two."

Ignoring my sarcasm she doesn't even pause before continuing. "Well, she's very good friends with Adeline Snow."

"The best-selling author of extreme sports romance."

"And also married to skateboarding legend Spencer Garrison."

My heart begins to beat faster. She's building up to something amazing and I can hardly take it. Spencer Garrison isn't only a famous athlete, but in the last few years he's really made a name for himself with his charities, especially in Texas. He's like some sort of philanthropic royalty.

Carrie leans in as if she's about to spill a huge secret. "It appears the happy couple is pregnant."

"No way!" I yell because that is, in fact, huge news. Not just in our little book community, but that's going to make national news.

"Yes way. And after much discussion, they've decided to give us the exclusive interview and announcement." Carrie looks quite pleased with herself when my jaw drops. "They're going to be in the area tomorrow so we're going to meet up and do a quick interview. I'll find out when they want this to go live."

I'm stunned. Well and truly astonished that the semi-super famous couple has chosen us to break the news to the world. It makes sense since they're pretty private and probably don't want this splashed all over whatever the newest gossip site is first. But for us, this is an opportunity to capitalize on new subscribers and new potential clients. A break like this doesn't happen every day.

We continue to discuss logistics and our vision for the final post when it goes live. It requires a bit of online searching for some pictures we might be able to use since there's no way we can afford a photoshoot. And of course during that search I run across a picture of Hunter on the red carpet last night. My heart plummets.

He's with his co-star, Penelope Warner, who looks amazing in her single-shoulder black Prada dress that only comes mid-thigh. His arm is wrapped around her waist as they smile for the camera. Gone is the lumberjack look and in its place is the version of Hunter Stone the world is used to. Hair perfectly styled, bright green eyes, and a perfectly tailored suit, he screams movie star.

Logically, I know they're probably just friends. I mean, he called me yesterday, and told me about the event. Knowing about it doesn't lessen the sting of seeing him with her. It just drives home how vastly different our lives are. Something that leaves me feeling sad and disappointed.

It's probably better we never defined our relationship. Or friendship. Whatever it was. It never would have worked out between us in the end. If it stings this much after only having him for a few days before he left, I don't want to imagine what having my heart broken by Hunter Stone would have felt like.

Chapter 21

Hunter

Normally I'm not a fan of running on a treadmill. I hate feeling like a hamster on a wheel, never getting anywhere. I prefer getting my cardio outdoors in the fresh air. I would have done just that this morning watching the sunrise while I managed to get in a solid five miles. But I overslept after too many restless nights and very little sleep.

Thankfully, my condominium complex has a state-of-the-art gym, and at this time of the day most of the residents are off at their high-powered jobs and not using the gym. At least I'm by myself and don't have to ward off anyone trying to make small talk. The music in my earbuds should distract me from my thoughts; I should lose myself in the beat as my feet hit the rubber belt. I don't. My thoughts are on the number of days since Celeste and I have spoken. Something feels off with her. With us.

I know better than anyone how busy she is with the play. Her job is not only time-consuming but can be emotionally draining. My obligations have kept me busy too. Adding in the time difference and we have hardly spoken on the phone more than a handful of times since I returned to L.A.

As late night turned to early morning, I thought about staying up a few more hours and calling her. Catching her before she could get to rehearsal. Instead, I must have fallen asleep because when I woke my phone was in my hands and covered in drool.

Glancing at the clock on the wall, I realize I've been at this longer than planned and start decreasing my speed to cool down. Lifting my water bottle to my mouth, I take a long pull as the treadmill ticks down before coming to a stop. Disconnecting my earbuds from my phone, I gather my things and place them on the counter before cleaning the machine and exiting the gym.

Today I'm meeting Matthew for lunch since he's in town for a seminar. I still have trouble reconciling that the guy I met on a photo shoot is a financial advisor by day. Actually, I never gave much thought that there was a day job. I really do live in some sort of Hollywood bubble.

Entering my condo, I toss my things on the breakfast bar and move to the master bathroom for a shower. Completely on auto pilot, I go through the motions before I towel off and wipe the mirror of steam. With two days off from shooting, I've allowed myself to not shave. It isn't quite the lumberjack look I have going but I'm still pretty scruffy.

Pushing off the counter, I quickly add a little styling cream to my freshly trimmed hair and brush my teeth before slipping into a pair of jeans and a black T-shirt. I may look casual, but the price of these jeans is more than I used to make in a month at my first job. It's ridiculous how expensive the simplest things can be and how easily I slid into spending the money without a second thought. Is that what it means about how Hollywood changes a person? Spending a few days in Celeste's shoebox apartment reminded me of how far I've come. I only hope I haven't lost myself in the process.

When I return to the kitchen, my phone vibrates on the counter.

Matthew: Are you still cool to meet for lunch?

Me: Yep. Heading out now.

Matthew: NOW? We said 1.

Laughing, I shake my head as I type out a response.

Me: Yeah and you're walking to the restaurant. I'm fighting traffic.

Matthew: *face palm emoji*

Slipping my phone in my pocket, I exit the condo and make my way down to the garage. When I signed my contract as a cast regular on Prince of Darkness, I treated my family to a vacation and my parents to a few gifts I knew they'd never buy themselves. The one purchase I made for myself was this truck.

My dad had one like this when I was a kid. Of course, his was a basic model without a single luxury. Yet, I remember him pulling it in the driveway, proud to have driven it off the lot with less than fifty miles on it. I promised myself that one day I would have the same feeling. The only difference: my feeling was amplified by leather seats and a kick-ass stereo system. It was my one true indulgence. Minus the overpriced jeans, of course.

I'm not overly frugal but I also know that all of this could end at any time. It's why I prefer to invest in things like my condo and not expensive watches and a garage full of high-end sports cars. I should probably pick Matthew's brain today about how else I can make the most of my investments.

"Call Celeste," I instruct my phone. The line begins to ring as I merge onto the freeway. The traffic is moving at a steady pace, slower than the maximum speed but at least we aren't stopped.

"Hello? Damn I need to do cardio."

Her breathless rambling makes me chuckle. "Hey. Did I catch you at a bad time?"

"If only you were here to catch me. I'm about ready to pass out from running."

"Why were you running?"

She doesn't respond immediately, instead I can hear her taking deep breaths and exhaling a few times. There may be a few swear words in there too. I don't dare tell her I just ran a few extra miles over my morning plan.

"I had my phone in my bag and was on the other side of the room. I didn't want to miss your call."

That statement makes me smile. It seems she misses me as much as I miss her. It also makes me rub my chest because of the ache I've been trying to ignore for days now.

"How's everything going?"

"Yes, Manuel. I'll be right there," she says before turning her attention back to me. "I swear that man wouldn't know what to do without me. Everything is good. Well, it will be. You know how this part of the process is. Chaotic, exhilarating, and exhausting."

"I remember those days. Hey congratulations on getting the exclusive on your blog. I saw it mentioned in a few articles. I'm really proud of you."

"Thanks." I can hear the smile in her voice. "It's been a little crazy. I mean, I knew Adeline Snow and Spencer Garrison were famous in our world, but I had no idea they were to the actual world. Hold on, Hunter."

The timing of her distraction is actually perfect as traffic and I meet again. I slow to less than a snail's pace as I listen to Celeste talk to someone in the background. The line is muffled so I know she's pulled it away from her mouth to speak. When she returns to the line she's giggling. I can envision her smile as she does and wonder if her wild hair is loose and free or piled on top of her head.

"Sorry, crisis handled."

The reality of how busy she is hits me and I feel guilty for keeping her from her job. "I'm on my way to meet Matthew for lunch."

"Oh really? That's cool. I'm sure he's as blissfully happy as his wife. I swear she hasn't stopped smiling since they got back from their honeymoon. Enjoy that sappiness in person."

"I'll be sure to report back to you."

"I'm sorry, Hunter. I have to go. We'll chat soon, okay?"

"Yeah oh—"

Before I can finish my sentence, the line goes dead. Like I said, something's off.

"Man, I'm so glad to be out of that conference for a while and into the sunlight." Matthew closes his eyes and tilts his head up to the sun. "I know I'm good at my job, but holy shit. People in the finance industry can be soooo booooring. They just drone on and on about numbers, their pasty white skin practically glowing."

"Talking about math all day sounds like my worst nightmare." I chuckle as the waitress drops our plates of food in front of us. "I'm almost surprised you didn't get hit on. I bet you were the tannest and most in shape of anyone there."

He grabs his napkin and shakes it out before dropping it on his lap. "I try really hard to ignore anyone attempting googly eyes. Years ago I made that mistake once. It did not end well. Besides, I'm fresh off the best honeymoon ever. Well, except when Carrie got in an argument over pet adoption."

"She wanted to adopt a pet internationally?"

"She wanted to adopt an Australian *possum*. You should have seen her arguing with the guy. I really think she wanted to bring one home."

"A possum?"

Matthew nods as he takes a bite and chews his food, a twinkle in his eye as he tells me about Carrie's efforts to adopt a rodent. Or whatever possums are. The only point of reference I have are the ones that used to sit on the wall behind my parent's house and stare at us in the dark. Creepy bastards.

"Your wife is a little crazy."

"Nah, she's passionate about animals. Especially any with a disability."

I'm still trying to wrap my brain around the idea of them having a pet squirrel and now he adds in the possum tidbit and I'll never look at Carrie the same again.

"Enough of that. I've been instructed to get the real story about you and Celeste. Carrie thinks she's holding back and is worried about her."

Choking on my burger, I swallow and take a drink from my beer before clearing my throat and giving him my attention. "Worried why? Is something wrong? She's been a little distant and I figured it was because she's tired from the production."

"Relax. She's fine. My wife, gosh I love saying that, anyway, she just worries about Celeste. It's hard for her with them being so far apart. They are the closest of friends but most of their time together is virtual."

"If you're sure. Maybe I should call her again."

I begin to shift in my seat, checking my phone for a message from her. Matthew has me worried.

"What went down with you two anyway? I know you snuck off during the reception and spent that last day together after we all left the resort. Then when Eddie called me after he couldn't reach you for a week, I knew something else was going on."

Will he believe me if I tell him I have no idea? Because it's the truth. There's more to it, but we didn't have enough time to figure things out for ourselves.

"We're friends."

Matthew chuckles lightly and shakes his head. "I think you're a cool guy, Hunter, but I'm friends with Celeste too. And I don't think I'd be as stressed as you obviously are at the mention that she may be in some sort of trouble. Admit it. You like her."

Scoffing, I reply, "Of course I like her. She's cool. We're friends." And I have no idea why I'm downplaying my feelings. This isn't an interview where I need to be careful with my words. This is Matthew Roberts. My friend. He's more trustworthy than a slimy reporter. Still, I fight to hold back because I just don't know.

"Mmhmm. And?"

"And what? We spent time together. I had some time off after the wedding, so I hung out with her in New York. I got some much needed rest. That's it."

"If you got so much rest why do you look like shit?"

Ignoring his comment, I take another bite of my burger and watch as he pulls up his phone and begins tapping away on the screen. Matthew is silent for a few minutes, clearly concentrating on whatever he's looking for on his phone. It allows me enough time to think of a new topic of conversation. Finances. That's as far away from this conversation of feelings as we can get. Instead, he continues beating a dead horse before I can swallow.

"I've known Celeste for a while now. She's part of the package with Carrie. Her and Luke. And Jamie. Damn my wife has a big circle. Anyway, when we were going through our wedding pictures, Calypso said this was her favorite. She said these two people looked really happy together."

Turning his phone my direction, I look at the screen and my heart jumps. I expected it to be a picture of him and Carrie. Maybe them saying their vows or their first dance. Instead, it's me and Celeste. We're both a few drinks in, that much is obvious by the red cheeks we're both wearing. With her in my arms, we're looking at each other, smiling as we dance under the white lights and moonlight. Her arms are draped over my shoulders and I can almost feel her fingers weaving through my hair.

"Maybe I'm overstepping but right now you look like shit. Celeste looks sad. Neither of you look like the two people in this photo. I know it's none of my business but if I've learned anything in the last few years it is that when you find the person who makes you want to be better, who brightens your days without trying, you'd be stupid to let that go."

His statement doesn't require a response and honestly, I'm not certain there is one. Comparing my relationship with Celeste to the one he has with his wife is like comparing apples to oranges. But I can't deny I understand what he's getting at and it leaves a lot for me to think about.

Chapter 22

Celeste

"Do you have the rehearsal schedules for every-one?"

I'm barely listening to Manuel rambling off instructions to the cast, instead absentmindedly doodling on my to-do list. The extra ink is going to drive me crazy later, but right now the fidgeting is helping me feel more anchored. Carrie's words about how love works keep running through my mind.

For the last few weeks, honestly ever since Hunter left, I've had this weird out of control feeling. For someone like me who prides herself on schedules, lists, and staying on task, feeling all over the place isn't a comfortable feeling. Fidgeting on a piece of paper seems to calm that anxiety for whatever reason I don't want to think too hard about. However, it also comes with the unintended consequence of distracting me from my job. Could Carrie be right? Am I brokenhearted? Is that why I'm so absentminded?

"Celeste."

"Hmm." I look over at Manuel, who is sitting next to me at the long table we use for rehearsals. I use it to take notes and whatever else Manuel needs. He uses it to house about a dozen empty paper coffee cups. I really need to bring him a travel mug every day.

"Are you okay?" he asks as I jot down the word "travel mug" on my to-remember list.

"I'm fine. Why?"

"Because I've asked you twice for the printouts of our rehearsal schedules." He's not angry with me. But he does look concerned.

I give him a half smile, face flush with embarrassment at being called out for my lack of attention and pat his arm in an attempt to smooth things over. "I'm fine. A little off today but nothing a good night's sleep won't fix. Here." I hand him three dozen copies of our schedules that have been organized and color coordinated according to importance—green for the leads, blue assigned to the understudies, and orange for the general cast. Eventually, I'll email the entire production a final version but until then, we need everyone to confirm there aren't any conflicts.

As with most artsy-type jobs, pay is low at this phase of production, so most of us have a second job to bring in enough money to pay the bills. Fortunately for me, most everyone in this cast works in a restaurant at night so creating an itinerary for daytime hours was relatively easy. I'm grateful for that. I've seen some calendars that were really wacky when a main actor had a day job. Talk about scheduling conflicts.

Fortunately, my mood has not affected my mad organization, and nothing needs to be changed. Except maybe my attitude.

I try to tune back into the conversation as they go over some blocking for a particularly vital scene, but my thoughts continue to wander. It's not that I don't enjoy working on this production. I really do. The play is well written. The cast is so very talented. The skeleton crew that's starting to build the sets are fantastic. Even the producers are relatively chill compared to others I've worked with in the past. The problem isn't anything to do with the job. All my feelings are because I made a big mistake.

I brought Hunter to work with me for the first couple of days and now all the memories that flood my mind when I'm here are of him. Hunter reading through lines and following Manuel's blocking instructions. Hunter laughing with one of the producers, who still doesn't know he wasn't just some scruffy wannabe actor but a bona fide movie star. Hunter winking at me when he caught me watching him from across the room.

It all happened just feet from where I'm sitting and because of it, the loss of him is heavy. Which makes no sense since we were together for such a short amount of time. There were no expectations and no rules. Just two people getting to know each other and liking what they found.

And now he's gone.

I try to remember that while he's off walking red carpets with beautiful coworkers, I'm back to eating Ramen noodles and slogging away, riding the subway every day. Our lives were just too different for anything between us to work out. That's what I need to stay focused on.

Well, that and work.

Rehearsal finally wraps up and I smile as brightly as I can while Manuel gives me last minute information he needs sent out to the crew on some potential changes to the set. And then I'm alone again…

walking down the streets of Manhattan…

riding the subway to my stop…

meandering toward my building…

opening my front door…

"Hi honey, you're home!" Anna yells around a mouthful of Ding Dong, her trusty guitar lying carefully on the coffee table.

"Where did you get those?" I ask as I close and lock the door behind me. "Are those Hunter's?"

She shrugs in indifference. "If there is food in my apartment, I will eat it. Besides, he still owes me from that Twinkie incident."

"He bought you a brand new super-sized box." I drop my bag on the floor and plop down on the couch, beginning the process of removing my shoes.

"And it was a good start. But he still broke my roommate's heart and for that he must pay."

I freeze, one shoe almost all the way untied, wondering how she came to that conclusion. "He didn't break my heart."

She shoots me a look and says, "Okay." Her tone means she's not buying what I'm selling.

"What? It's true." I continue getting rid of my shoes because I may be wearing sneakers for safety and comfort, but that doesn't mean my peepers don't hurt after a long day.

"Then what's with the moping around lately?"

I scoff. "I have not been…" Yet another look that means I can't lie to her. I sigh. "Fine. You win. But I wouldn't call it heartbroken. We weren't together long enough for that. I think. It was just a fling so maybe just disappointment."

"You mean *heavy* disappointment."

"Fine," I concede.

"So heavy you mope around all the time."

"Fine. Okay. I get it. I'm a grump and I'm difficult to live with."

Anna holds her hands up in front of her like I'm the one who started this whole thing. "Whoa there. Calm your tits. I didn't go that far with my assessment."

I sigh and drop my head onto the back of the couch, arms wrapped tightly around my bent legs. "I promise

I'll be fine. It's just taking me a little bit to get over the loss of him being here. I think maybe the emotion of it all is a little unexpected so it's taking me a little longer to push through this weird feeling. It's also making me hungry."

I snatch up the box of Ding Dongs and pour the last one into my hand with a maniacal laugh as she protests.

"I was going to eat that!"

I shrug. "If it's in my apartment, I'm going eat it."

"Touché, my dear friend." Cramming the last bite of her faux cupcake in her mouth, Anna grabs the box and begins breaking it down for the trash. "You know what else I do when I'm feeling down in the dumps?"

"What?" I take a bite and moan in delight. She's right. I should have been emotional eating all along.

"I write."

And I choke on my bite.

Not concerned by my impending death, Anna calmly hands me the glass of water she has on the table and I drink down its contents quickly, just trying to stay alive.

When the Ding Dong is finished trying to kill me, I'm finally able to speak. "I don't know what you're talking about."

"I think you do. There is a manuscript that's been sitting on this table in that exact same place for close to a year." She points and waves her finger around.

"It is not," I argue. "Hunter moved it over a bit."

Anna smacks my leg lightly. "Seriously, Celeste. That screenplay and that dumb convention were the only things you talked about for like two years. They were your goals, remember? You finally made it to the con and came home with the best kind of parting gift, if I do say so myself." She waggles her eyebrows making me huff a small laugh. "Why aren't you working on that second dream?"

I shrug sheepishly. "I have writer's block."

"And now that you're an emotional mess, you might find yourself unblocked." She grabs the notebook off the table and tosses it on my lap. "And if not, it won't hurt to get some of your feelings on paper. Many great stories have been written because someone opted to write for free instead of pay for therapy."

With those parting words, she grabs her guitar and heads to her room, closing the door quietly behind her.

I think about what she's said and how getting my emotions on paper might be the key to getting out of this funk I'm in and unlocking my creativity. And then I remember Hunter's words.

"Maybe you're stuck because your passion is plays over movies."

And then it hits me and as Anna predicted, the wheels start spinning with solutions to every corner I've written myself into. The entire story plays out in my brain like it's happening in front of my eyes. Quickly, I grab a pen out of my bag and flip open the notebook, frantic to get everything on paper before I forget.

Taking a deep breath, I put my pen to the paper and write.

And write.

And write.

Chapter 23

Hunter

It's been a few months since the wedding in Turks and Caicos. Months since I've overindulged in whiskey. There's a reason I don't do it often and last night's events would be why.

My most recent go-around didn't lead to laughter, long talks by moonlight, or a beautiful blonde. No, last night I gave in to my shitty mood and exhaustion and drank until I could see the bottom of the bottle and then passed out. On my couch. In my underwear. Aren't movie stars sexy?

Unlike the morning after I drank a little more than I usually do with Celeste, today I woke up feeling like a truck ran over me. Then backed up and did it again for fun.

Dog shit. I feel like dog shit. But, at least I finally

slept and didn't have dreams of the East Coast and a different life.

The shower I took and the greasy bacon and egg sandwich I scarfed down this morning didn't help but at least now my pounding headache is more of a low rumble. That is thanks to the empty bottle of children's rehydration drink sitting on the table.

Now, my future sits before me on the table. The same table my proposed contract with Prince of Darkness has been sitting on since I returned home. A stack of papers waiting for me to sign my life away. Or at least commit to three more seasons with the show. Every provision I asked for has been met and then some. Apparently when I wasn't looking, Eddie added in a few stipulations that would allow me to dip my toe in the producers pool as well.

It's everything I wanted and some of the things I've only dreamed of. Yet, I can't seem to sign it. That was a contributing factor to my drunken weeknight. The stress of these decisions weighing heavier on me than I let on. At least I've learned to keep this type of behavior to the confines of my condo. Or a tropical island where I know there isn't any press.

Eddie expected me to scribble my signature on the dotted line without a second thought. Truthfully, I did too. This is what I've worked for. This is why I've sacrificed a life. To get a contract like this. The series is hotter than ever and unbeknownst to the public, the plan is to go out on top with these next three seasons being all that remains. Other shows have done this in recent years and the move has catapulted not only the ratings but the actors to the next level.

It should be an easy decision. And still I continue to ignore the document and the decision. The idea of being committed to the show for years to come seems daunting. Stifling.

The ringing of my phone draws my attention from the show I'm watching, which incidentally is not at all vampire related. As I reach for the phone, I mute the television.

"Hello?" I greet without looking at the screen.

"My son is alive. Thank goodness. Daniel, we can stop printing the missing posters!"

My mom has jokes. "Very funny."

"I thought so. Your nieces and nephews think I'm quite funny. Perhaps since you've missed Sunday dinner more than you've made it, the fact that I'm quite the comedienne has escaped you."

Ah yes, mother's guilt, we meet again. I'd almost forgotten what it was like to be on the receiving end of her passive aggressiveness. Paola Stone is forthcoming and outspoken when it comes to most everything. Except when it comes to laying on the guilt. That she saves for casual and sometimes dramatic comments.

"I'm sorry. I promise to be there this weekend."

"What's going on, Hunter?" Her tone softens from one of reprimand to genuine concern. That almost makes me feel worse. "You're busy, I know that, but you've always made time for your family. It's been months since we've seen you."

Sighing, I don't respond immediately. With my head resting on the back of the couch, I rub my forehead, a tension headache fighting to make its presence known. Or maybe it's the lingering effects of whiskey. Who's really to say?

"Honestly, I don't know. I feel restless and indecisive. I'm staring at the contract I've worked so hard for and I'm not sure I want what it offers."

"Oh honey. How long has this been going on?"

That's the million-dollar question. I want to say since the trip to the wedding and the weeks that followed. I want to blame the hesitation on exhaustion. Truthfully, it's been a gradual shift over the course of the past year. I've become more restless, wondering what direction to take my career. What the next five years looks like. Who I want to be a decade from now. Will I still be happy being an actor or is there more out there for me?

"Maybe a few weeks. Maybe a year. I'm not really sure. I just know there's something holding me back.

Like the fixer she is, Mom begins talking through it to a solution. "What about asking for more time? Can you do that? Take a break and think things through?"

"No. I've already put them off until Monday. Eddie is breathing down my neck for an answer. And, before you say it, he isn't pushing because of his commission. It's more that I haven't been able to explain my inability to commit."

My mom doesn't respond immediately. Instead, the line is quiet, only the sound of the television in the background. I hear a door close and then the telltale sign of her windchimes and I know she's settling into her favorite chair on the back deck.

When we were kids my mom would sit in that chair and read books, drink tea with her sisters, and watch us kids run around the yard. She's always called it her oasis and over the years my dad has worked hard to make it extra nice for her. Once I started making real money, I pitched in to the fund to upgrade everything. Well, except the chair. That has remained the same.

"Hunter, you're holding back. That's concerning to me. We've always been able to talk about anything. Level with me."

I sigh deeply and do my best to speak without thinking too hard. Maybe that'll get to the crux of the problem. "I should be over the moon. I'm doing what I've always dreamed of. I'm an actor. A *paid* actor, Mom. While I'm not wealthy by any means, I'm most definitely not hurting. We've seen my name in big lights with my first major picture. It's almost impossible to go to a big box store because I'm recognized. Still, even with all of that happening, it feels like something is missing. How selfish does that make me sound?"

"Oh Hunter. It isn't selfish. If anything, it means you have bigger dreams than even you realized. For you it has always been about your craft and never about popularity and money. When was the last time you were truly happy?"

I don't hesitate to respond. "When I was in New York."

"Oh my, back when you were picking up change off the ground and surviving off the care packages we sent you?"

Chuckling, I stand from the couch and move to the kitchen for something to drink. "No, Mom. Give me some credit. I mean, those were great days and I thought every experience was the absolute best. But I meant a few months ago after my trip to my buddy's wedding."

"Ah, the trip to the tropics and the weeks you fell off the radar. What made that time different than the rest?"

Celeste. It's the simple answer with the most complicated connotations. Being with her relaxed me. Balanced me. Working with Manuel as they put the production together and feeling that energy zipping around the space was intoxicating.

"Hunter? Have I lost you? Dammit, is this thing charged?"

I stifle a laugh as I hear her voice get loud and then quiet. I know she's pulling the phone away and looking at the screen.

"I'm here. I was just thinking."

"Phew. The kids were watching some videos on it last night and I thought maybe it killed my battery.

Talk to me, honey."

She makes it sound like we're going to talk about the weather or what to buy my niece for her birthday. Something simple. Something casual. Celeste is anything but simple and casual.

"I met someone."

"In New York?"

"Before New York but she's who I stayed with while I was there. We actually met months ago at one of the big Cons. Then as luck would have it, we were both at the wedding, and then…"

My mom sighs into the phone. It isn't a sound of frustration but one that reminds me of my sisters when they were teens and crushing on a boy. It's the sigh of a hopeless romantic. Of a woman who has been married to the same man for more than half her life.

"And then you fell in love."

Choking on nothing but the air I breathe, it takes a few minutes for me to gather my wits enough to reply. "I never said anything about love."

"A mother can hope. So tell me about her."

That I can do.

"Celeste is great. She's a total theater nerd and pretends she doesn't watch television, but I found her secret obsession with Prince of Darkness, although she swears she was only watching to critique my character development. Her laugh is infectious, and she is kind to everyone. Her roommate is a little scary and a lot outspoken, but they have a great yin and yang thing going."

"And being with her is what made you happy?"

"Yes and no," I answer truthfully. "It was everything. Not being committed to being in ten different places in one day. The reality that I could get lost in a city and just be me. Be us. We walked the streets together without being approached, went out to dinner like regular people, and then she took me to the theater. That's when I remembered why I wanted to be an actor. Why I love this industry."

The line is quiet again but this time, I welcome the silence. I'm left to sit in my thoughts. To recognize the truth in everything I've said.

"And Celeste? She's part of this too, isn't she?"

"Yeah. The time we've been apart has been harder than I expected. We didn't talk about what happens next, just living in the moment. But, now, I keep looking at this contract wondering when I'll be able to see her. She's building her own career, and I can't ask her to come here, even if it is for only a few days to visit."

"Well, that sure is a lot to unpack. So I understand, you met a woman who you spent time with and want to continue to spend time with. Someone you care deeply for and who, I assume, also feels the same about you. Meanwhile, your career is at a level you've worked for and have finally reached but still doesn't feel fulfilling. Is that about right?"

When she puts it like that I feel like an idiot. A

whiny idiot. I have a great life. I'm blessed beyond my wildest dreams and still, I don't feel fulfilled.

"That's about it. What advice do you have for your favorite child?"

"You know I love all my children the same. Do not play that game with me. You're a smart guy, Hunter, you don't need me to share any words of wisdom. I think deep down you know what you need to do. Just remember you became an actor because you love being on the stage. It's where you're comfortable and your true self comes to life. No amount of money or fame will matter if you don't love what you're doing. I look forward to meeting the woman who has made you want to put your heart above all else."

"Thanks, Mom."

"Anytime, honey. Now I have to go see if your father has fallen asleep in his recliner. We'll see you Sunday at six. Love you."

"Love you too, Mom. Thanks."

Ending the call, I take my drink and resume my spot on the couch. Picking up the contract, I read through it one more time. This time, I look at it with different eyes and my mom's words floating in my head. Slowly, it all becomes clear.

"And you're sure I can't change your mind?"

Shaking my head, I reread the terms one final time

before signing my name. Replacing the cap to the pen, I place it on top of the papers and slide it toward Eddie.

"We've discussed this. Stop looking so crestfallen."

"I'm worried about you. This feels so sudden and out of character."

Laughing, I lean back in the chair, my hands behind my head. "It's actually completely within my character. I just forgot for a while who I was. I'm not quitting acting, just adjusting things a bit."

He picks up the contract and stares at it wistfully. He's so much more distraught about this decision than I am. That explains a few things. "You know, this is probably going to send Prince of Darkness fans into a frenzy. They won't know what to do with themselves. Nikolai the crime fighting vampire in only six episodes a season."

"They'll survive and so will you. I owe my career to this show but it's time for me to get back to basics."

"Please. We know you mean getting back to the girl."

He has no idea how true that is, but this decision is also about what is best for me. For my soul and how important acting is to keep me centered. Besides, Celeste has no idea I'm doing this. I wanted to tell her but each time we've spoken it never felt like the time. Maybe I'm a wimp or, perhaps, I'm scared she'll discourage me from making this change. Or that she'll simply reject me.

"If she'll have me. Now come hug it out with me and wish me well. I'll be back in a few weeks to shoot that episode, and I'm still expecting you to follow up on that indie film."

Eddie grumbles but rounds the conference table and pulls me in for a hug. If I'm not mistaken, he sniffles. Oh jeez, he's crying. I've got to get out of here. Cutting the hug short, I smack him on the back and exit the room. Waving to the receptionist on my way to the elevator, I scroll through my contacts. I know I saved it here. Or at least I thought I did. Shit. I didn't. Great now I have to scroll through my texts for our conversation.

The trip to the garage level is quick but it's enough time for me to find the conversation I was looking for. Sliding behind the wheel of my truck, I back out of the space and when I pull out onto the street, connect the call. Dammit. I didn't even think of the time. Oh well, I can leave a voice—

"Hello?"

"Manuel? It's Hunter Stone."

"Hunter? Oh! Hey. Gimme a sec."

Flicking my blinker, I turn to the onramp of the freeway and merge into traffic. The line is quiet for a few seconds before Manuel comes back on the line.

"Sorry about that. This is a… wow, yeah. This is a surprise."

"I know. Sorry to call so late."

"No bother. I'm a night owl. What can I do for you, Hunter?"

"I'm going to be making a move back to your neck of the woods and wanted to reach out."

Why do I feel like I'm asking a girl out on a first date? I'm so nervous.

"Of course you are. It is the greatest city in the world. Hollywood isn't for you."

Laughing at his candor, I reply, "You have no idea."

"Celeste hasn't mentioned anything, I'm sure she's thrilled."

"She doesn't know yet. I planned to surprise her but before I do, I wanted to see if you know of any productions casting? I'd like to give my agent a little nudge in that direction and it would help if I can hand him some potential auditions. You know, get him less heartbroken about my television exit and more excited about the Broadway potential."

This time it's Manuel who laughs. A very loud and boisterous laugh at that.

"As a matter of fact, I think I know of a production in need of a leading man. When do you plan to arrive?"

"I'm on the red eye Sunday."

"Text me your itinerary and we will meet next week. And don't worry—I'll let you break the good news to Celeste."

Chapter 24

Celeste

Rehearsals have been going well. The cast gets along, the skeleton crew is quick and understands Manuel's vision down to the details, and I'm checking off items from my lists by the hour. The producers are pleased with the progress we've made in a short amount of time and other than the occasional meeting, haven't been around much.

The biggest snag is our main actor. And by "snag" I mean major crisis. Two broken bones in his ankle and surgery to place pins means he's can't walk for a minimum of six weeks. And a main actor that can't walk means he's out of the show.

No one is blaming him for being injured in a freak accident. From what I've been told, he has been taking a dance class, which is pretty common when you're a stage actor. That and singing lessons give you more marketable skills. What's not as common is missing a landing after a leap. I don't even want to think about how he managed breaking two bones. Just thinking about it makes me shiver. This is why I prefer to work behind the scenes. No leaping permitted. I hope he recovers and wish him well, but his accident has put us in a precarious position.

Thankfully, Jeremiah, the understudy from the ensemble, has really stepped into the role with ease. Not that he wouldn't. It is his job after all. Still, it doesn't really help the production overall. Jeremiah is the best at playing several small characters because his face is like rubber. His innate inability to morph from character to character seamlessly has made him a vital part of the cast. Don't misunderstand, Jeremiah could be a great lead. But he is a phenomenal character actor. A true standout. What we need is another actor familiar with the script and able to slide into the lead role. But that is a pipe dream. And since we're so far into pre-production, it's going to be next to impossible to recast.

The whole thing is a mess. A fixable one but a mess just the same. The most concerning part is Manuel's reaction to the issues. He has been extra cool about the whole thing. It is completely out of character from the usually dramatic and well… over-the-top director. I'm worried he's going to crack at some point. A director that loses his shit is a much harder predicament to come back from than losing a character actor to the lead role.

"Okay, people!" Manuel shouts and claps his hands together a couple times. "We've got work to do. Let's pick it up where we left off yesterday. We're in Act One, Scene Three."

He strolls back to the table where I'm already sitting, going through my to-do list and responding to emails.

"Anything I need to be aware of?" he asks me quietly as he sits down.

"We have a tentative opening date." I turn my laptop so he can see, and he smiles at the news. We both know the date is pending producer approval, but this is a good sign that we're still on track despite the setbacks.

"Awesome. Can you do me a favor and go let the costume design team and set crew know about this?"

I furrow my brow. "You don't want me to just email them, so they have it in their records?"

"You can do that too, but I'd feel more comfortable if I knew they were told in person. Just to make sure there's no confusion about our deadlines."

That's weird and not at all our usual process. Maybe this is his way of dealing with the stress of the cast change. It's not really my place to question so I say, "Sure," and head out of rehearsal, hoping I don't miss something important.

The walk to wardrobe isn't long. We're all in the same building but they've holed up in a room at the far end of a narrow hallway. The space is huge, and they've lined it with large workspaces, mannequins, and sewing machines. So many sewing machines that all you hear when you enter the room is a constant hum. Although not nearly as fancy as that of major motion pictures or even televisions shows, it's a great setup for a theater with our budget.

"Hey Cheryl," I greet as I sidle up to the lead designer's workspace.

"Hi Celeste." She pops the end of a piece of thread in her mouth before squinting her eyes to thread a needle in her hand. "What's going on? Did Manuel have another design idea he needs right away?" She laughs softly because ever-changing details are part of his charm and reputation.

"Actually, no. We have a tentative opening date and he wanted to make sure it won't mess with your schedule."

Cheryl looks as confused as I am but shakes it off quickly. It only takes a few minutes to give her the info and make sure we're all good to go. Then I'm out the door and on my way to set design.

The conversation there is almost identical, except Sal doesn't look at me strange. He doesn't look at me at all, instead continuing his work. Although he does pause to say, "Is Manuel losing his shit? Because I've never missed a deadline yet."

After reassuring Sal no one was losing their minds, except possibly me on this weird expedition, I'm off and hustling back to the room. I don't like missing out on rehearsal. I'm always afraid something major will happen, I won't be there to notate it, and it'll fall through the cracks.

Fortunately, I've only missed about ten minutes and it doesn't seem like they've gotten far in my absence.

"Break's over!" Manuel yells.

Break? They took a break at the beginning of the day? Maybe Sal's onto something about Manuel's mental state.

"Uh… let's switch gears." Manuel flips through his script until finding what he's looking for. "I want us to start in Act Two… let's do Scene Five."

Act Two, Scene Five? That has a major monologue for our lead. A lead who hasn't rehearsed that with only Manuel yet. We've intentionally skipped over this scene because it is so complex with emotions.

"Let's do the monologue."

My jaw drops open. What is he doing? Looking around the room, it appears I'm the only one surprised by this turn of events. The actors are moving around, shuffling positions with not a care in the world that our director is currently in the middle of a mental breakdown. Maybe I'm in a bad dream. That would make more sense than what is actually happening.

Taking a deep breath, I try to just go with the flow. None of this is what we had originally planned for today and I have no idea what's happening. But if I know anything about working with Manuel, it's that he always knows what he's doing, even if I can't figure it out.

I flip my laptop back open and go back to my emails, keeping an ear open to everything around me. Scrolling, I almost miss it. The low timbre of his voice. The way my skin peppers with a chill as he speaks the first words.

"She's wrong. No matter how much my mother beats into my head that my ideas, no, my dreams aren't good enough, I have to remember, she's wrong."

Holy shit. It's Hunter. Hunter Stone. *My* Hunter.

He's here. In the room. The man who has invaded my dreams and captured my heart is here standing in the middle of our rehearsal space reciting the monologue from Act Two, Scene Five.

I lean closer to Manuel. "What is happening?" I hiss, totally confused.

"Shhh." He waves me off. "I'm trying to concentrate on our new leading man."

"Our what?" I screech before smacking a hand over my mouth.

He shushes me again and leaves me no choice but to turn back to Hunter, who has taken one step closer. My heart is beating so hard, I'm sure it can be heard by the cast. Oh boy. So fast. Am I breathing? Yes. In for three and out for three. I watch and listen as he recites the words I've heard for weeks but never felt like I do in this moment.

"My life has been unfulfilled. Dreams are nothing without believing I can make them come true. The problem is, my mother wasn't wrong."

Wait. That's not his line.

I grab the script and flip quickly to the right page to see if I missed a change.

"In fact, my mother is the one who reminded me of my passion. The person who finally convinced me to get it right."

I skim quickly.

Nope. No changes. He's gone off script. Manuel isn't stopping him and no one else is confused. What is he doing?

Looking from the script and back to Hunter, he seems closer than he was seconds ago.

"My world isn't complete. My dreams aren't in Hollywood. My desire isn't to rule the small screen. My mother was right. My passion is right here in New York City."

Hunter takes another step forward. His eyes are locked on mine. There is no hesitation as he speaks. No fear in his voice. But I'm afraid. Terrified to hope he's here, not just for the theater but for me.

"Being an actor is what I've always wanted to be. But somehow in the process I lost who I am. Then I met a wild-haired blonde, with her lists and calendars, who reminded me of what's truly important."

Oh yeah. He's totally off script now. Unless this is

a different play than I signed up for, which isn't a bad thing. I like this new version. It is starting to sound more like real life.

Taking another step closer, Hunter continues. "I'm an actor. Always have been. But, it wasn't until I came here with you that I realized I can be the man I want to be."

Behind Hunter, just over his right shoulder, I spot Jeremiah. He has a huge smile on his face as he sashays dramatically to my side and reaches his hand out for me to take.

I chance a quick glance at Manuel who is smirking as well. It finally hits me that he set all of this up. His unnecessary task to personally talk to Cheryl and Sal, who I assume are also co-conspirators, so Hunter could sneak in makes more sense. His lackadaisical attitude about our injured leading man makes sense since he's already hired Hunter.

The puzzle pieces fall together in my brain. Hunter is moving to New York and now I'm being wooed by him.

I have a quick fangirl moment where in my head I scream, "OHMYGOD I'M BEING WOOED BY HUNTER STONE!"

But then I look up and all I see is Hunter—the man who changed my life and inspired me to follow my dreams and maybe, just maybe, be the love of my life.

Taking Jeremiah's hand, I let him escort me to center stage, or center room, where Hunter is waiting for me. As I approach him, I note the way he inhales slowly, his hands fisting and flexing by his side. Hunter Stone is nervous.

Standing in front of him, I bite my lip with my own insecurity. Could this be real? Is he really here for me? The questions in my brain are endless as I wait to see how this plays out. But when Hunter takes my hands in his, a calm comes over me.

"Celeste, I left before we could talk about us. That was one of the biggest mistakes of my life."

I suck in a breath. That's not what I was expecting him to say, but I like hearing it.

"It's been a few years since I've been around someone who likes me for me. Hunter the guy who eats too many Ding Dongs, enjoys a good egg sandwich for lunch, and mixes up his Tylenol with Ambien."

In the background I hear someone say, "I bet there's a good story to that one."

I ignore them, totally focused on the man in front of me.

"When I'm with you, I feel like I can be myself totally and completely. And I want you to feel like you can be totally and completely yourself with me."

He pulls us closer and that's when I feel the tears begin to prick my eyes.

"If you've already moved on, I'll understand. I should have thought through more carefully what I was doing, but I hope that what we have isn't only one-sided. I left before I could tell you how much you mean to me. I want nothing more than to be with you. In front of all these people, I'm asking you Celeste Puh… mker," he mumbles the rest of my last name, not even coming close to the pronunciation. "So, I'm asking you, in front of all these people. The same people who better not be making a secret video to sell to the paparazzi or I'm not holding up my end of the bargain and I won't be springing for drinks tonight."

"Don't screw this up for me, I'm poor! I need free drinks!" someone yells and the rest of the cast laughs. I don't blame them. It makes me giggle too, the extra squint in my eyes forcing the tears down my cheeks. Hunter gently brushes them away with his thumbs.

"If you've moved on and all we can be is friends, that's okay because that's my fault. But if you are willing to take a chance on me… on us…" He pauses and takes a deep breath, probably to squelch his own nerves. "I'm falling in love with you, Celeste. It started the moment you handed me that playbill, and it's only grown with every minute we spent together and every minute beyond that. So if it's okay with you, I'd really like to be with you. Only you. If you'll have me."

At this point, I can't stop the tears. They just keep coming. And then the laughs begin. And before I know it, my arms are around his neck and I'm hugging him as tightly as I can as I laugh and cry, cheers and applause breaking out around us.

"I'm falling in love with you too," I say through my tears. Even with the noise around us, I can still hear his sigh of relief.

We pull away, still smiling and all the questions I have start pouring out.

"Are you really staying?"

He nods, still holding my hands.

"But what about Prince of Darkness?"

He shrugs sheepishly. "I renegotiated my contract to only shooting a few episodes every season so I can make New York my home base. And when Manuel told me this part unexpectedly opened up…"

I whip my head over to gape at Manuel, who winks at me.

"… It all just fell into place."

"I bet the producers were thrilled to hear the fabulous Hunter Stone joined the cast," I tease.

He smiles shyly. "They may have mentioned something about the marketing being much easier now."

I scratch at the scruff on his face. It's not as long as it was during our vacation, but it's nice to see he's letting himself relax more. I can already tell this transition is the right thing for him.

"There's only one problem."

I furrow my brow. "What's that?

"You never did get your interview."

I smile. "I don't need the interview. I got something even better."

"Yeah?"

"I got you."

I reach up on my tiptoes and kiss him, not even caring who sees.

Chapter 25

Hunter

Two years later

I'm too young for heart palpitations. Right? I'm barely in my thirties and yet, I'm pretty certain it's time to call a cardiologist. Who knew being a producer would be the only role I've played that sends me into a panic?

I've been live on national television, presenting our industry's highest award and didn't have the level of nerves I do tonight. Opening night on Broadway. My mom told me it is because this isn't about me. This is about Celeste. My amazing, talented, and beautiful girlfriend. She may be right. Watching your own dreams come true is much less nerve-wracking than watching the one you're in love with reach theirs.

Celeste's play turned out so much better than I anticipated, and as soon as I read it I knew it would be perfect for Broadway. I immediately started making calls and after utilizing some of the contacts I've made over the years, I found quite a few theater influencers who agreed.

I know it's practically unheard of for an unknown play to make its debut under the big lights of the most iconic stages in the world, but if anyone deserves it to happen, it's my girlfriend.

I watch Celeste as she stands before a member of the press. Confident and completely in her element as she smiles and talks to the people who are bombarding her with questions. She amazes me. When I reassessed my life a couple years ago and took a leap of faith that she loved me as much as I loved her, I had no way of knowing how much our lives would change.

Coming back to New York was the single best decision of my life. In the two years since I relocated, Celeste and I have moved in together and settled into domestic bliss. Well, as much bliss as a guy who likes to lounge around in his underwear reading scripts and a woman who lives by lists can cohabitate.

Only blocks from her old apartment with Anna, our place is newer and bigger. Thank goodness. I'm not a small guy and that shower of theirs left a lot to be desired in the way of space. While my girl originally balked at the idea of my paying our rent, she relented when she saw the second bedroom I had turned into an office. It was in that room that she put the finishing touches on her play. The same story she was originally determined to make into a screenplay. I'm not sure what changed her mind about that part, but I like to think I had something to do with figuring things out.

"Hunter!" The reporters are relentless. As much as I try to stay in the shadows, they won't leave me alone. Too bad for them, my eyes are only on Celeste.

Rolling her eyes, she nods her head for me to join her. Taking a few steps, I stand beside her, wrapping my hand around her waist and plastering that Hollywood smile I perfected long ago.

"Hunter. Congratulations on all the Oscar buzz. You must be thrilled!"

This is why I was standing in the background. I didn't want to take away from Celeste's night. The independent film I worked on last year has been cleaning up at the film festivals. The buzz for the film, the director, and even my acting is all anyone can talk about. There are whispers we'll be up for the biggest award in our industry. I'm not holding my breath, though. This industry is amazing but it's also fickle. Anything can happen.

"Jacqueline, you know I don't listen to the gossip. Tonight is about Celeste and her hard work."

"And yours. As producer, this is as much your night as it is hers."

Inhaling, I flex my hand on Celeste's waist, but she shifts so her hand is on my chest and her eyes capturing mine. Her smile centers me, diffusing the frustration I feel. Keeping her body flush to mine, she turns only her head back to Jacqueline.

"You're right. Tonight is a dream come true. What writer doesn't dream of having their story come alive? But all I did was write the play. Hunter and everyone else involved in this production deserve all the credit. We've been so blessed to work with such amazing people. It's truly an honor to stand here tonight with all of these talented people as all of our hard work comes to fruition."

If I didn't already love this woman more than I thought was humanly possible, I'd be a goner right now. Not only did she selflessly give credit to everyone in the production, she put the woman trying to make this about anything other than Celeste in her place. I can't wait to get her home and to our bed where I can fully show her how much she astounds me.

Thanking Jacqueline for her time, we move down the red carpet, stopping for photos when prompted. The press in New York is a far cry from what I experienced in Los Angeles. Eddie was right, Prince of Darkness dominated the ratings the last two seasons and my limited appearances have somehow made it the show to watch. Viewers have been chomping at the bit, hoping my character, Nikolai, will appear. Which is what has made it almost impossible to spend any time there. The paparazzi are absolutely relentless. New York may be a bustling city, but somehow I still get to live at a slower pace here.

Thankfully my family accepts my gifts more easily than my girlfriend and have gladly taken my plane tickets to come for visits. Even Eddie has spent more time on the East Coast, making rumblings of moving his family here for the culture. Personally, I think it's the pizza and hot dog trucks that pique his interest.

When we approach a reporter I recognize, a couple turns to exit the interview spot and I realize it's my buddy Jonah. When he sees my face, he does a double take before offering me his hand and pulling me into a hug.

"This is fucking crazy, man. Who knew New York would be more pumped for a red carpet than Los Angeles?"

"Jonah, good to see you. It's a different vibe here for sure. You remember, Celeste, right?"

Nodding, he accepts the quick hug before my girl turns her attention to his wife. When his attention is back to me, I ask, "How's it going? I didn't expect to see you here since you never called me back after we talked about that script."

"Oh that P.O.S.? I passed on it. You were right, it was a mess, and we'd spend more time rewriting than shooting. I'm still in post-production in that drama I told you about."

"Still?" I ask as someone nudges me to the side. Our foursome moves, allowing the next group to step up for an interview.

"Yeah. I can't seem to find the right song for the arc. It's one of the reasons we came here. I'm supposed to meet a few producers and see if there is some untapped talent I'm missing out on."

Talent. Untapped. I may have what he needs. Slipping my phone from my pocket, I pull up Anna's page on the Literary Arts website and copy the link before texting it to him.

"Take a look at that. It's Celeste's best friend, and she's ridiculously talented."

Nodding, he thanks me and then excuses himself and his wife. Celeste and I wait for our time with the reporter. Then, she does exactly what I expect and why, even though I'll never admit it, she's my favorite reporter.

"Celeste Pumperkin, it's a pleasure to meet you. Tell me about this dress. It's to die for." Never once does Barbara Wells give me the time of day. No, her attention is on the woman of the night and nothing makes me happier.

"Help me. If I have to take another step in these death traps, I may die."

I chuckle at her antics. "Babe, I'm the actor. It's my job to be dramatic, not yours." Celeste smacks me in the arm as I bend down to slip off her shoes. Lifting her feet to my lap, I massage the arches while the car creeps through Manhattan traffic and in the direction of our apartment.

Sighing, she settles into the opposite end of the seat, her eyes closed and a look of pure bliss on her face. The drive isn't too long but enough that I think she's fallen asleep. When the car comes to a stop she groans and shifts her body, slipping the shoes back on.

I thank the driver and lead my girl into the building. We take the elevator to the third floor and exit, walking hand in hand to our apartment. Well, I'm walking. She's hobbling. The moment she steps into the space, Celeste kicks off her shoes and makes a beeline for the kitchen. I follow suit, shedding my tie and jacket along the way. When I reach the island, I lean against the counter, my eyes on her as she rummages through the refrigerator.

"What are you doing?"

Never turning to face me, she says, "Getting food. I'm freaking starving. I think… yep here we go." Pulling a storage bag with leftover pizza from the shelf, she unzips it and takes a huge bite of a slice, making me chuckle.

Taking a step forward, I steal a piece from the bag and leave her alone to satisfy her hunger as I move through the space to our bedroom. Moving quickly to my dresser, I glance to the door to confirm I'm alone before opening the bottom drawer. Most people would hide a small square jewelry box in the top drawer but I'm not taking any chances. Celeste isn't nosy but with my luck, the one time she puts laundry away she'd find my surprise. Sighing in relief that the ring is still nestled in its place, I close the drawer again and whisper, "It's almost time and then you will make your debut."

I have no shame that I'm talking to a ring sitting in a drawer covered by my rattiest t-shirts. Truthfully,

I check on the box a few times each week. I've not wanted to take away from all that Celeste has worked for with the production by adding an engagement to her already lengthy list. So, I've waited and when the time is right, I'll know it.

Stripping out of the confines of my suit, I hang it in the closet before going about brushing my teeth before Celeste joins me. Gone is the bag of pizza and in its place, signs of exhaustion from the night.

"Did you finish off all the pizza?" I greet her as I pull her flush to my body.

"No. I left one slice. I'm not a monster."

Placing a quick kiss to her lips, I step aside to allow her access to the bathroom. Once I'm settled in our bed, I wait for her to join me. It isn't long before she exits the bathroom wearing only a pair of panties and a tank top. Goddamn. She's gorgeous. Her hair is down, wild and loose like I like it. I can make out the silhouette of her curves beneath the tank and I have to remind my dick she's exhausted.

When she yawns and climbs into bed, cuddling into my side like she does every night, I scoot down, resting my head on the pillow. We lie like this for a few minutes, neither of us speaking, just in the moment.

"It's hard to believe we moved in together a year ago."

I smile and drop a kiss to her head.

"Thank you, Hunter."

"For what, babe?"

"For believing in me. In us."

Slipping out from our position, I face her, pushing a stray curl from her face. "I should be thanking you. Not only for this life but for including me in your professional one. I'm sure there's a romance author out there, just waiting to write our story. It would be a best seller."

Leaning forward, she places her lips to mine. "It'll never happen."

"Why?"

"Because, our real life love story is better than the book."

Then she kisses me again, proving she's right.

Chapter 26

Anna

These dogs are going to be the death of me. Literally. If I don't trip over their damn leashes and land in the street, run over by a cab, I'll die of boredom. I tried putting in my ear buds and listening to music early on in this gig but then I couldn't hear the assholes growling at passersby or each other. I swear, they say these little dachshunds are supposed to be sweet and cuddly. They, whoever "they" are, well, they're liars.

It's fine. This job is only temporary. And necessary if I want to make rent on time. Which I do. Especially since I've once again lost a roommate.

Since Celeste moved out, I've had three people come and go. I understand having a nook in the corner as a bedroom isn't ideal, but you would think starving artists would be happy to only have one roommate instead of twelve. Somehow I keep finding the people who underestimate how expensive city living can be and once again I'm back to covering rent on my own. I miss Celeste.

I truly am happy for her and Hunter. They're perfect for one another and I love seeing my friend happy. But her happiness means I am here, walking the streets of the Upper West Side with three little assholes named Alvin, Simon, and Theodore. Sadly, they are not sweet little chipmunks and none of them sing. I asked. I thought it was a funny joke. Their fur mommy wasn't amused.

Think positive, Anna. Focus on the things you can control. These little shits are not anything you can control. Your music. The site and your contribution. All things in your control.

Repeating my mantra, I feel my anxiety and stress lessen as I turn the corner and cross the street. Ever since I began writing for the Literary Arts website Celeste and her friend Carrie own, my own music has been getting more interest. The downloads of my original songs

have increased exponentially. Oddly enough, the interest started with the exclusive announcement Carrie had of some romance author and her skateboarding (and millionaire) fiancé's baby. She's a cute baby but I don't understand why people care so much. Not like they actually know these people.

Still, that increase also means as long as I keep up with my end of the bargain, they pay me enough to pay my electric bill every month. Beats the hell out of picking up another non-singing dog to walk.

Once the high maintenance trio are returned to their home and I've taken the train back to my tiny apartment, I bypass the living room and head straight for my room. Flopping down on my bed, I try to relax. A nap would be a good idea since I have a gig tonight. It's not the highest paying job, but it's playing my music before an audience and there's always a possibility that an audience member will be someone in the industry.

My feet hurt and I wish I had the extra money for a pedicure. These are luxuries I can't indulge in. Fingers crossed I can find a new roommate soon and get back to my old life of the occasional pedicure and actual Twinkies instead of the imitation brand. Damn. I wonder if I can guilt Hunter into buying me a box. Is my birthday coming up soon?

As I contemplate whether I need to add "No eating my Twinkies" clause to my roommate agreement, my phone vibrates in my pocket. Tugging it out, I open the notification.

> Unknown: I really like your music and would like to discuss using one of your songs in a movie.

I roll my eyes. Like I believe this is an actual person. is this the new telemarketer game? I'm not a sucker.

"Joke's on you buddy," I grumble as I toss the device onto my bed next to me. It immediately vibrates again.

Unknown: I'm not a creep or fake.
Really. My name is Jonah Eriksen
and I'm a director. Hunter gave me
a link to your stuff. It's really
good and I'd like to discuss a col-
laboration.

Okay, now he, or she, no need to be sexist, has my attention.

Me: How do I know you're legit?

The three dots bounce only seconds before the response comes through.

Unknown: You don't but I am. Hunter will vouch for me.

Uh huh. And I'm the Queen of England. Actually, maybe Princess Margaret from *The Crown* is more accurate. I've never really followed the rules.

Still, I have Hunter's number. It would be stupid of me not to at least ask him.

Me: Some guy claiming to be a director texted me. Says you gave
him a link to my music. Am I being
punk'd?

It only takes him a second to respond.

Hunter: Yeah Jonah said you were
giving him shit. He's legit. We've
worked on movies before and he's
trying to find a new artist so he
can feature their music in his up-

coming film.

I sit straight up in bed, jaw wide open in shock.

Me: Holy shit are you serious?

Me: Also you owe me a box of Twinkies for making me think I had a crazy stalker coming after me.

I shrug at myself. Unlikely he'll fall for the guilt trip, but it's worth a try. His response is quick.

Hunter: LOL. You spelled "thank you" wrong.

Hunter: Also, you're welcome.

Yes, yes I am welcome.

Holy shit. I might break into the music industry after all.

We hope you loved Better than the Book, next up is Beyond the Lyrics.

Acknowledgements

With every book we write, we try very hard to make it as accurate as possible. There's always license for some creativity, but that doesn't mean we don't want it to be true. We never could have given Celeste a theater job without help the ever fabulous **Maegan Abel**. Thank you for letting us pick your brain and for guiding us with terminology on those fine details only a true industry professional would know. Celeste is better for it!

Megan Addison there are no take backs. You're stuck with both of us. Sure we forget what day of the week it is and you have to tell us how to find something at least seven times a week but WE LOVE YOU! Thank you for keeping us in line and tolerating us.

Allyson Murphy Don't think you can ignore our messages to read for us. We will find you! That was far less creepy in our heads. Moving along … Thank you for taking the time to help us perfect Hunter and Celeste.

Mandee Migliorelli jumped in at the 11th hour and made sure all our NYC transportation details were correct. Newflash: They weren't. Don't believe everything you read on the internet kids, especially when it comes to using the subway from Brooklyn. Imagine if we took our own directions. We'd be *in* the Hudson!

Karen Lawson is one of the only people who can handle us. We're a bit much on our own (we know it even if we pretend we don't) but together … whew! Your tolerance of the inconsistent ellipsis and commas is to be rewarded. Maybe with a glass (or three) of wine.

Mary Jo Lagoski is a fantastic set of last eyes. Somehow she always learns something new when she reads our books. Like how a poké roll isn't a sex position, no matter how romantic you make it. But then again, to each her own.

We know you're wildly impressed with our organization this time, **Alyssa Garcia**. You're welcome for not making you drink. Much. Now about that next book ….

Sassy Romantics, Carter's Cheerleaders and Nerdy Little Book Herd y'all rock the socks off us both. Not that we wear socks. I mean menopause is a thing and all that. We love you and think you are all the coolest book nerds around!

Lastly, **Deva Marie** and **Danny Montooth** have been the most fabulous narrating team to work with. Not only are they as invested in our books as we are, they desire to put out the best product as possible right along with us. Never could we have imagined we'd work with the absolute best of the best. Big things are coming for you both, if we have anything to say about it! Thank you for making this a collaborative project for all of us!

About the Authors

M.E. Carter and Andrea Johnston are romance writers who share a love of the written word. Combining their sense of humor, beliefs in love, and sarcasm, this writing duo has joined forces to create the Charitable Endeavors series. With the sole purpose of bringing laughter and love to their readers while tapping into their charitable hearts, a portion of the release proceeds will be donated to charity.

Other books by M.E. Carter

Hart Series
Change of Heart
Hart to Heart
Matters of the Hart
Matters to You

Texas Mutiny Series
Juked
Groupie
Goalie
Megged
Deflected

#MyNewLife Series
Getting a Grip
Balance Check
Pride & Joie
Amazing Grayson

Charitable Endeavors
(Collaborations with Andrea Johnston)
Switch Stance
Ear Candy
Model Behavior
Better than the Book

Smartypants Romance
Weight Expectations
Cutie and the Beast

Other books by Andrea Johnston

Country Road Series

Whiskey & Honey
Tequila & Tailgates
Martinis & Moonlight
Champagne & Forever
Bourbon & Bonfires

Military Men of Lexington

Promise Her
Cherish Her
Love Her

Standalones

Life Rewritten
The Break Series
I Don't: A Romantic Comedy
Small-Town Heart
It Was Always You

Charitable Endeavors

(Collaborations with M.E. Carter)

Switch Stance
Ear Candy
Model Behavior
Better than the Book

www.ingramcontent.com/pod-product-compliance
Lightning Source LLC
Chambersburg PA
CBHW071244190726
48292CB00007B/2395